# SCARY

## A Spine-Splintering Slide into What Lies Inside the Psychotic Mind

**Barbara Eck Tosi**

ARCHWAY PUBLISHING

This is a work of fiction. All of the characters, names, incidents, organizations, and dialogue in this novel are either the products of the author's imagination or are used fictitiously.

Archway Publishing books may be ordered through booksellers or by contacting:

Archway Publishing
1663 Liberty Drive
Bloomington, IN 47403
www.archwaypublishing.com
844-669-3957



ISBN: 978-1-4808-5632-5 (sc)
ISBN: 978-1-4808-5634-9 (hc)
ISBN: 978-1-4808-5633-2 (e)

Library of Congress Control Number: 2017919588

Print information available on the last page.

Archway Publishing rev. date: 06/08/2021

# For David,
# My Beloved Husband and Friend

I found you even though I wasn't looking.
You searched for me when I couldn't yet be found.
The Fates somehow sensed the emptiness we shared
and placed us together on solid ground.

You pierce my black darkness with your brightest light.
My bitterness you sweeten with your soft smile.
You know not to tame my wild and free spirit
as well as the quirkiness that is my style.

Your kindness permeates my hesitant heart,
and my restless soul thus finds a placid place.
Your confident shyness is one of many charms
radiantly reflected in your fair face.

You wear compassion like a well-tailored suit
as you render relief to those who know pain.
Your presence you freely with humankind share.
The sun from your spirit leaves no room for rain.

Your armor provides me peaceful pause from hurt
so that I, with new voice, may sing to the birds.
Your loving nature has given me reason
to, with childlike joy, unwrap my gift of words.

# Contents

# Mort

The embalming fluid floated in a fluted flask on top of the freezing table next to the stiff and chill-filled corpse, which was understandably unable to dissect the details regarding its righteously ripe, rigor mortised remains over which the methodical mortician held high his rigorously rigid reins.

The nervous night was ludicrously late but not too late to have to abort the perfectly precise postmortem plans of the meticulous mortician, Mort, who contemplated the cold carcass under the full moon's high-beam light, which so iridescently illuminated the corpse's considerably creepy plight.

The mortician inserted tubes into the cadaver to drain its lifeless blood, executing extreme efficacy to circumnavigate a bloody, behemoth flood. Beneath each thick and tensile tube, he securely situated a sturdy pail for the exceedingly rare but egregious event, the trustworthy tubes did flail.

After the corpse's blood had been delicately drained and duly collected, he then the precious pails with poised, painstaking precision inspected. With the blood's pomegranate patina, Mort appeared adequately pleased, so he next, the remaining blood from the tubes systematically squeezed.

Not one delicious, decadent drop of this exquisite elixir could be wasted, as this ripe, rich rendering would deliver divine drinks after being tasted by the voracious vampires, whose lusty thirst was quickly quenched when their throbbing throats with fertile blood were decadently drenched.

The vampires' hidden home existed far beneath the wooden floor, whose smooth and seamless surface concealed a secret trapdoor. By a rustic red rug, the trickster trapdoor had been cleverly covered, ensuring that the blood imbibers were not at risk of being discovered.

Inside craftily customized coffins, they silently slept away their days, dipped in dreamy, delicious darkness that detested the sun's bright rays. But as soon as daylight ducked beneath a new night that flawlessly fell, the coffin lids erupted, and vampire mouths soon began to swell.

After the trapdoor was lustily lifted, the vampires eagerly emerged and wildly walked across the floor as their tenacious thirst swiftly surged from their tantalizing thoughts of the rapturously ripe, ruby-red libations that would serve to sweetly satisfy their beastly and bloody expectations.

Mort poured and poetically presented this crimson-colored concoction in a prized punch bowl he had purchased at a *For Morticians Only* auction. Poised punch cups perched on hooks hanging from the red-stained rim of the antique bowl arranged on a table in the tasting room, deathly dim.

The perfectly positioned punch cups coaxed the greedy, gruesome grip of the vampires, whose large, loose, and lurid lips would satisfyingly sip and gulp, guzzle, and guiltlessly gorge on this necessary necrotic nectar, made so smooth and sumptuous by passing through a particle detector.

After the vampires lewdly licked the punch bowl and punch cups clean, they formed a long line that led directly to Mort's indoor latrine. Each of them wearily waited for the opportunity to expeditiously expel the luscious liquid that quickly caused their bladders to severely swell.

After unleashing ubiquitous urine, blatantly bloody and royally rich, they dripped their drool as they dipped their cups into a designated niche of the latrine and drank the urine, which was again later excreted after barbaric binge-drinking bouts that were with regularity repeated.

The blood they initially imbibed temporarily satisfied their twisted thirst, until which time, Mort magically managed some additional arteries to burst inside the hushed, blue-blushed, caustically cold and creepy cadaver, whose bountiful blood unfailingly filled each vampire's mouth and bladder.

Out of Mort's open office door, the revamped vampires willingly went, anxiously anticipating the deeply dark hours that would shortly be spent inside grisly, growling graveyards and on the horrifyingly haunted trail, where scary, sanguinary spirits were known to moan and woefully wail.

Before morning captured its clandestine chance to light their dismal path and disastrously deliver its blindingly bright and wickedly white wrath to Mort's office, the vivacious, voracious vampires reluctantly returned, and Mort suddenly something unusually unsettling about them discerned.

As they began to nerve-numbingly notice the needlessly neglected shelves, they alarmingly appeared not in the least to be their bubbly, bloody selves. They believed that Mort had been disrespectfully derelict in his restocking of bottles of blood that bolstered their bite and nefarious nighttime walking.

The vindictive vampires failed to fathom that, in the adjoining room, boxes brimming with bottled blood were boldly waiting to assume their proper places on sacred shelves that now sat brazenly bare because Mort's nap had lasted longer than any of them were aware.

With transparent tenseness, they thanked Mort in their vampiric way for faithfully feeding their fabled fetish for fresh blood from dead prey. They falsely flattered him on his fixation to furnish them sweet peace by endlessly ensuring that their dark desires dramatically found release.

They then insolently indicated to him that he'd grown forgetful and old and appeared troubled and tired and lamentably lacked the beastly bold grip that he over this bountiful *bed-and-bloodfest* had hypnotically held and explained that the time had arrived for his useless life to be quelled.

After they mercilessly mocked Mort for running out the reservoir of blood, their thorny teeth pierced his neck, and he fell to the floor with a thud. He was very dead, so they opened the trapdoor and descended the stairs and promptly proceeded to the protected privacy of their loathsome lairs.

Into their macabrely menacing coffins, the vampires predictably climbed, and with their herculean hands that were bloodied and seriously slimed, they easily enabled the cob-webbed covers to readily release and drop. Then they drifted into deep sleep and dreamt about blood nonstop.

On the upstairs wooden floor, Mort lay chillingly cold and motionless, as he morbidly marinated in his pathetically premature postmortem abyss outside the adjoining room, where big boxes of beauteous blood waited for Mort's attentive action that would forever remain radically belated.

The next day a new mortician would arrive at the site and officially be designated to drain the blood from incoming cadavers' every artery. Mort's corpse, of course, would be tubed first, so his blood could flow

and

fill

punch

bowls

for

the

vengeful

vampires

that

quietly

waited

below.

# Handpicked Lover

Professor Miller was highly esteemed and duly deemed an academic sage because he solved the perplexing puzzles that permeated each penned page of the considerably complex novels that his English literature class read—novels whose secrets were stoked when stroked by lively, literary thread.

The professor collected the ethereal thread during his much younger years. These specialized spools were the tools he used to allay his innate fears of misinterpreting the moods and methods of the famous authors he studied while he was still a college student with a brain undeveloped and muddied.

When the thread touched an author's text, the text began to eerily unravel the murky mysteries and tense themes that within the novels did travel. As the menagerie of meanings became unmasked, the students were prepared to explore the elliptical eccentricities that the thin thread effectively bared.

The many mixed meanings that the writers may or may not have intended, were exhaustively examined and evaluated by the students, who pretended to completely comprehend the curiously complex, confusingly cryptic forms commonly used by accomplished authors to create legendary literary storms.

Professor Miller entered the room and prepared to begin his lecture when his electric eyes locked with those of a student whose exquisite texture of whisper-soft, winter-white skin and luscious locks of long, silken hair quickly called to mind a Shakespearean maiden, the sweetest and most fair.

Professor Miller's literature lecture eventually came to an exuberant close, and his cultured class of creative collegians from their academic chairs rose. His eyes and those of the stunning student intimately intersected once more as she shyly, but seductively, leaned against the lecture hall's open door.

As she waited for him to make a move, he wildly walked toward her, both magically and momentarily blinded by the lure of love's lusty blur, which dramatically did their acute angles of vision undeniably impair, as they faced each other with eyes eagerly engaged in a sensual stare.

# Barbara Eck Tosi

After the crowded classroom of students had dispersed and dissipated, the two predestined lovers, with excited bodies undeniably unsatiated, to Professor Miller's palatial home without a hint of hesitation went, and there, they, the red-hot remainder of the delirious, delicious day spent.

They playfully pursued their passions upon the same bed that was shared by the professor and his wife since the day the two had been paired. Entwined like twisted, climbing vines, the professor and his lover decided to use to their maximum advantage every possible perk the day provided.

The professor's wife was out of town and would return in just a few days. He and the student made lots of love amid the summer sun's sizzling rays. Succulent juices sensually signaled their simultaneous orgasmic release, secured through shared stimulation that brought them both sweet peace.

Over the clandestine course of many months, these randy rendezvous continued to avidly arouse them both without arousing any clues that could calamitously cause the sudden eruption of significant suspicion about this blatant betrayal now in free-falling and full-fledged fruition.

The student lover was acutely aware that Professor Miller was married, and one day, as they in each other's bare bodies were very deeply buried, she told him he must immediately confess their love affair to his wife and divorce her so the inseparable lovers could commence a new life.

Professor Miller gazed at his young mistress and feigned a loving smile, assuring her, they would soon walk together down the marital aisle and that he would, that very night, reveal his transgressions to his wife and demand her full agreement to terminate their miserable married life.

Upon hearing his promise, the student provocatively professed her love, but suddenly and shockingly was severely struck from high above. Her head was heinously hammered with a huge, heavy candlestick, which categorically and completely killed her in a manner chillingly quick.

# SCARY

Professor Miller had savagely snuffed out her young, inexperienced life, which ensured he would not be forced to forfeit his unsuspecting wife. Although he'd stopped loving her long ago, he still depended on her money, which, inside her bulging bank vault, marinated in sweet cream and honey.

The professor carefully cut off one of his lifeless lover's lovely hands—a ritual that resonated as one of his sick, self-imposed, signature demands after murdering each of his handpicked and ludicrously luscious lovers, who, for many years, he had luridly lured beneath his silken bedcovers.

Of the dead students' hands, he had amassed quite a colossal collection, and with the macabre lot, he proudly portrayed his professorial perfection, by turning them into paperweights like those of famous mystery writers, whose scary novels satisfied the most notoriously nervous nail-biters.

He hid his prized paperweights in a wall safe located inside his den. These trophies were identified with strokes from the professor's pen. He quirkily kissed and creepily caressed them as he so fondly remembered how his student lovers had looked before he had their hands dismembered.

The professor proceeded to roll the body inside an heirloom braided rug and then began the student's one-handed corpse to the cold outside to lug. He dragged the rug across his front yard, all the while looking everywhere to make sure a nosy neighbor was not of his most unusual behavior aware.

He lifted the blood-besieged rug and placed it into the trunk of his car, and after driving several miles, he dropped it into a dumpster not far from the college dormitory where his student lover had lived and studied before he sadistically struck her head and left her very dead and bloodied.

Upon returning home, Professor Miller bundled up the bedroom bedding, placed it inside his car's bloody trunk, and then began hurriedly heading to the nearest Laundromat so he could wash out the sick and sinful stains caused by lethal lovemaking and blood that leaked from arteries and veins.

He stuffed the blood-soaked bedding into an oversized washing machine, a front-loading, see-through version that promised particularly pristine results after he agitatedly added ample amounts of stain-seizing soap that guaranteed the reborn bed linens could pass inspection by the pope.

After the industrial-sized washing machine had been satisfactorily started, the professor, from the nightmarish Laundromat, in a glazy daze, departed. He walked next door to eat his lunch at the popular Grille and Fryer, after which his laundry would likely be ready to do time inside the dryer.

His taste buds teased by a picture of a cheeseburger, milkshake, and fries, he ordered the tantalizing trifecta, looked out the window, and did realize that outside the Laundromat, sirens sounded, and red lights were flashing. This startling sight sent the paranoid professor to the Laundromat dashing.

Professor Miller opened wide his eyes to confirm that he wasn't dreaming as armed officers pulled their weapons and the patrons started screaming. The professor thought that soap fumes might have made someone fall ill, or an impatient customer had died while waiting for a slow washer to fill.

The professor asked befuddled bystanders, who were busy milling about, the reason for this mysterious mixture of mayhem muddled with doubt. The police, he learned, had a female college student's body discovered, but her body was missing a hand, and that hand had not been recovered.

When the Laundromat owner called the police to report a hand she did see inside a front-loading washing machine, where a hand should never be, the officers immediately realized that they were one step closer to finding the killer's closeted identity, which was now very quickly unwinding.

The police, sidestepping sadistic suds, swiftly searched the slippery scene and solidly secured the entire building by locking every door and screen. The throbbing throats of screaming patrons became inflamed and tight. Huddling together near the exit, they remained fraught with feral fright.

# SCARY

The perplexed professor looked at the washing machine that he was using. Through its glass front, he saw something that was alarmingly accusing. A dismembered hand's palm creepily clung to the inside section of glass as the maniacal machine mechanically made each surreal and sudsy pass.

Warning words written on the hand's palm with a permanent black marker, caused spines to splinter as this sinister scene grew significantly darker. The words that immediately identified the English literature student's killer

were

convincingly

confined

to

these

very

chilling

two:

"Professor

Miller!"

# The Blizzard and the Can Opener

A blinding blizzard was brewing as the old woman sipped her cup of tea. She somehow knew that its biting blast would reach her precisely at three o'clock that afternoon, so like a career circus performer on stilts, she rose to the ominous occasion by collecting candles, matches, and quilts.

Her psychic prediction came to fruition later that day when she looked out her cottage's kitchen window, where she spotted the winter-white rainspout. The rainspout was always red and meticulously matched the little red shed where her little calico cat cozily slept inside her little red calico cat bed.

The little shed was still red, but the *always red* rainspout had turned *white.* This catastrophic change in color caused the old woman to fill with fright. Her body stiffened from sudden shock, and her soul was soaked with fear from her rapid, rattled realization that the end of the world was very near.

Ancient folklore eerily espoused that the *white* rainspout horribly housed a hellish history that, when the Fates were, by deadly desires, aroused, repeated its truly terrifying tale in seismically spine-splintering displays that terrorized the trembling trumpets on these diabolically dark doomsdays.

A white rainspout was described within the pages of an ancient sermon as an exceptionally evil entity whose belly bulged with vicious vermin. A white spout signaled that snow was on its very scary and wicked way—snow whose apocalyptic power few could decrease, destroy, or delay.

The old woman locked and bolted the doors and placed aside her knitting, then took an inventory of the canned goods that in her pantry were sitting. Except for her little calico cat, she lived a simple life in her cottage alone, without the noxious and noisy nuisances of a television, radio, and phone.

The little calico cat loved to play with what skittered and slithered outside, and the little red shed provided a perfect place for her to both eat and hide from formidable forces that she was unable to scare away or fight—like the always red rainspout whose crimson color had become snow-white.

# Barbara Eck Tosi

The startling sight of the white rainspout, as declared by those now dead,
predicted a brutal, bellicose blizzard with a hellishly herculean head
that would, like a volatile, vomiting volcano, hiss, howl, belch, and burst,
and kill those whose meager food supply was cause to have them cursed.

Those who lacked enough food to last through the snowstorm's end
would die within three days and not another day of life ever spend.
People who had food enough for the duration of the barbarous blizzard
would be spared suffocation by snow by the benevolent Blizzard Wizard.

The old woman's cache of canned goods fully filled her pantry shelves
but stood no chance of being opened unless they opened themselves.
Unfortunately for her, the collection of cans was the old-fashioned variety
that depended on a can opener to set their solidly sealed contents free.

Sadly, she only owned one can opener because of the frugal life she led.
That can opener was the crucial key to keeping her alive and fed.
Looking out her kitchen window, she glimpsed the winter-white spout.
It was three o'clock, and a brutal blizzard was blowing snow all about.

Ten feet of snow had already fallen, and the unsettled sky remained littered
with ferociously falling fatal flakes that surreally sparkled and glittered.
The snow had mustered a momentum that caused the old woman to doubt
that to this inevitable, world-ending Armageddon, there would be an out.

In her well-worn wooden rocker, the weary, worried woman somberly sat
with winter mittens on her hands and on her head a warm woolen hat.
Three days later, slumped in her rocker and wrapped in her favorite quilt,
she dismally died inside the cottage that her loving late husband had built.

Her little calico cat lay fatally frozen inside her little red calico cat bed,
next to crystallized cans of cat food that were neatly stacked in the little red shed.
The old woman's only can opener upon the cold-corrupted cans lay,

where

she

had

lamentably

left

it

to

her

dark

and

depthless

dismay.

# Wednesday Afternoons

The mysterious man was strikingly strange and lived alone in his home, which madly mimicked a morbidly morose and monotonously monochrome hideously haunted house of horrors on a relentlessly rainy, raucous night when surprised spines are severely splintered upon seeing a spooky sight.

He was quietly and covertly cloistered inside his house most of the time, and to his unusual existence, there seemed no rational reason or rhyme. A spry sprint of a squirrel was one of few movements to indicate that anyone inhabited the property behind the rusted, wrought iron gate.

Every week the man was seen climbing into his large van and driving to a neighborhood grocery store whose food kept him alive and thriving. He predictably pursued his grocery shopping every Wednesday afternoon when he hurriedly and hungrily headed to the ever-popular Looney Tune.

The Looney Tune was his favorite food store, just a few short blocks away, where he serially shopped and seriously stocked up on the awesome array of supremely sumptuous staples that would satisfactorily see him through to the next Wednesday afternoon when he would again the same thing do.

The man was always alarmingly hungry each time he in the store shopped, and that is the real, raw, ravenous reason his weekly trips never stopped. The Looney Tune was unequivocally the uniquely perfect place where he could his hellish hunger easily, expressly, and ecstatically erase.

He earnestly enjoyed the music that played throughout the grocery store. It was this mood-mystifying music that the Looney Tune was famous for. The food, to be sure, was farm fresh, top shelf, and considerably cheap. The alluring aisles were wildly wide, and the shelves were deliciously deep.

Each Wednesday afternoon, the man parked his large van in the same spot, which was located behind the Looney Tune in a very vacant lot. He always entered the grocery store through a rear door that opened into a men's bathroom, which subsequently led to the store and its lively crew.

# Barbara Eck Tosi

It was Wednesday afternoon, and he settled inside the Looney Tune to shop. His succulent spree soon started when he caused the cashier to fatally drop to the linoleum floor below the cash register where, mere moments before, the psycho wielded a hatchet that killed him in a scene of grisly gore.

After checking the cashier off his list, the man struck down the stock boy, who, for such a sadly short time, had enjoyed his part-time employ, stocking cases of canned goods on the sturdy shelves of the Looney Tune until dying from hatchet-induced hemorrhaging on this dreamy day in June.

The man wandered behind the fresh meat counter to certifiably verify that the butcher he had just attacked did undeniably very dead lie. He butchered the butcher close to the bone so as not to create any waste. Being thoroughly thoughtful, he saved some scraps for stray dogs to taste.

The buxom, boisterous baker, who sported a sugar-white baker's hat, now after being hacked with an anxious ax, slumped lifelessly over a vat of ridiculously rich, righteous, and royalty-worthy red velvet cake batter, her bludgeoned body decadently decorated with red-rose-colored blood spatter.

A woman who, for twenty years, had worked diligently in the deli was smeared on the floor after being pureed like just-made juniper jelly. The man annihilated her body in a manner so madly methodical and divine that she could easily be spread on crackers and enjoyed with a robust red wine.

His victims' raw, repulsive remains the monstrous man carefully lifted. He situated them inside his sagging shopping cart as it steadily drifted toward the rear edge of the eerily empty Looney Tune grocery store, through the men's bathroom, and, ominously, out the store's back door.

How, one might ask, were this madman's deeds able to go unnoticed every Wednesday afternoon inside this fabled store that was fully focused on furnishing fresh food and mesmerizing music that excitingly elicited serene states of mind in the song-savvy shoppers that very regularly visited?

The shoppers were distracted, that is why, by the tunes that dizzily danced inside their inattentive heads while the man upon his victims advanced. As he discretely managed to carry out his murderous and messy shopping, the cleaning crew converged in the assaulted aisles to commence their mopping.

They postulated that the pools of human blood were spilled spaghetti sauce that burst and broke their jars, causing major mayhem and a profit loss. It was all the crew could do to mop up the mess and bring out more cases to restock the empty shelves and wipe clean their sauce-splattered faces.

Why, one might ask, was only a pathetic, paltry piece of attention paid to the disturbing number of missing persons' reports that had been made by the restless relatives and faithful friends of the shoppers who had failed to return home from the Looney Tune after their lives had been derailed?

The police were already so overwhelmed with their cache of cold cases that this prevented their penetrating pursuit of the twisted and tangled traces of missing shopper information that far below a thick pile of files did lie. That remains the straight, simple, short, honest answer to the question *why*.

The man loaded his selections of fresh food into the back of his large van, double-locked the door, jumped into his seat, and very quickly began the short stint to his home where this wicked, wretched, and brutal beast would immediately upon his gory, gruesome groceries festively feast.

And when his sadistic, shark-like feeding frenzy had finally ended, this maniacal man's deeply demented mind very pathologically pretended to forget the nutty name of the silly song that had so many times played inside the Looney Tune where his human groceries he had just splayed.

Why didn't the store owner inspect his surveillance cameras every day? And why did the Looney Tune staff continue to offer themselves as prey? Simply suffice it to say that some mysteries in life are better left unsolved, and some serial killers are never found, and their sins remain unabsolved.

It was Wednesday afternoon, and the man was again at the Looney Tune. One by one, he murdered his grocery items and planned to be home soon. The song he had pretended to forget was now playing and finally set free

its

title:

"Never

Go

Grocery

Shopping

When

You're

Hideously

Hungry!"

# Archway of Ice

Pensive pine trees purposefully punctuated a formidable, forbidden forest that disgustingly displayed its hellish horror even when the very poorest natural daylight dimly dappled each dreadfully dark and deadly pinecone that dangled dangerously and danced deceivingly within this devil zone.

Two side-by-side rigid rows of curiously contained and crystallized trees, with barely enough room between them for a small-sized soul to squeeze, inwardly bent their ice-bundled branches, thereby creating a crisp canopy that formed a literal *archway of ice* that guarded its menacing mystery.

The frozen forest's frosty features faultlessly framed the archway of ice, which possessed a palpable, pulsating power that very plainly did entice a doggedly determined college junior to enthusiastically enter it, despite knowing that only a select group of people had been awarded that right.

The permission to enter the archway of ice had always been solely reserved for seniors who sought to ensure this ritual for them alone was preserved. Those persons who gained entrance without these necessary credentials would be forced to face a frightful fate notorious for nefarious potentials.

The daring, disobedient ones, who at this revered rule blatantly balked, would, until the moment of their dastardly death, be sadistically stalked. One curious and courageous college junior rejected everyone's advice and walked through the irresistibly iridescent, inauspicious archway of ice.

Beneath her weighty winter boots, the glassy ice did splinter and crack as she, flaunting her fearless focus and fixation, never once looked back. Although her fierce free spirit prevented her from feeling any remorse, nothing and no one could protect her now from a fateful lack of recourse.

After she willfully walked through the archway and exited the other side, a mean-looking man drove close to the street curb and successfully tried to scare her with his cold, creepy, cemented, and deeply demented stare before he pulled away and discretely disappeared into the eerily ethereal air.

## Barbara Eck Tosi

After attending her literature class, the student began the treacherous trip back to her dormitory, all the while attempting not to slide or slip on the dicey, ice-covered sidewalks, streets, back alleys, and glaciated ground where *very bad things* did lurk and hide and were quite unexpectedly found.

The student stepped up her steady stride and had but one block yet to go when the seriously strange man once again his foul, fearful face did show. He prudently parked his ugly van next to the edge of a crystallized curb, much like a needy, nondescript noun nudges a verifiably vibrant verb.

During the daytime, a deluge of dirty laundry the man dutifully collected, and later, after it had been professionally cleaned and officially inspected, he delivered it to the same loyal, long-time customers so that they could dirty it again and for these time-saving services, continue to pay.

As the lowlife leapt from the van, he ghoulishly and guiltlessly grabbed the college student, whose body he suddenly and systematically stabbed. When she was attacked, she started to scream, so he slit her tender throat and slashed her body so severely that she soon in a blood bath did float.

He effectively inflicted at least thirty wounds, all without any time gaps. Afterward, he devilishly drove at least thirty vicious victory laps around the dormitory, where the female student had most recently resided as her brazenly butchered body in the laundry van back and forth glided.

His work shift had almost come to an end, so he then proudly proceeded to the cleaning service's command center, where he immediately needed to dispose of the student's discombobulated corpse in the exact way that his barbaric, bloodthirsty boss had instructed him to do every day.

He arrived at the company headquarters, where he for years had worked. The man dragged the dead student's body to a location that lustily lurked somewhere between his boss's office and a closet full of cleaning supplies where all *archway of ice dissidents* ultimately met their diabolical demise.

## SCARY

The mad, monstrous, maniacal man dumped the student's rotting remains into a long, narrow chute, where he witnessed her brutally bruised brains disgustingly disengage from her fissured, fractured, fragmented female skull and hideously hit the insane incinerator's hellishly hot interior wall.

Despite being dead, the college junior appeared on TV the next day in the cleaning company's commercial, where her ashes were on display. Company commercials were creatively crafted by select staff on day duty, whose responsibility was to perfectly prepare the previous night's booty.

The laundry staff rubbed the dead student's ashes into a clean white shirt so that tantalized TV viewers could plainly see the despicable dirt before the super, stain-assaulting solution was shaken and amply applied. After this application, the shirt was spotless after being washed and dried.

These commercials cleverly caught and kept the female viewers' attention and often prompted them this conscientious cleaning company to mention to the women within their social circles who just very well might contact this service to make their clothes commendably clean and bright.

Each day, this same strange man with the cold, creepy, and convoluted stare returns faithfully to the fearful side of the newly named *Archway of Scare,* where he watchfully waits for the next non-senior college student,

whose

inevitable

death

will

plainly

prove

that

breaking

rules

is

never

prudent.

# She, MD

Her dedicated years of scholarly study had delivered great dividends along with accumulated accolades from her ardently academic friends and her family, as she had become a surgeon who confidently could filet fresh flesh with instruments like those that now before her stood.

The sedated patient, who on the stainless steel table did securely lie, was surrounded by sterile surgical staff set to strictly abide by the savvy, scalpel-sharp surgeon's illustrative and intricate instructions based solely on sound science and her medically meticulous deductions.

The male patient was scheduled for a simple, standard hernia repair, and therefore, the skilled surgeon and her able assistants were aware that his low-risk, routine surgery would most likely go wonderfully well and not come even close to triggering a surgical room emergency bell.

Seriously scrubbed and gallantly gloved, the surgeon stole a swift glance at the patient's eerily familiar face as he lay in a temporary trance. Her psyche was simultaneously struck with severe, spine-splintering fright, as she readily recoiled after recognizing him in the surgery room's light.

Her skittish subconscious and hellishly hot hatred took a terrifying turn as monstrous memories of this wildly wicked man in her brain did burn. Suddenly a nurse's frantic voice on the hospital intercom pleaded for personnel to report to the ER stat, where they were desperately needed.

Saturated with severe, sudden shock, the surgeon ordered her staff to run and informed them that *she* alone would remain behind to handle *this* one. She could rapidly repair hernias in her sleep, and this man required little surgical prowess to make him feel fitter than a fastidiously tuned fiddle.

The entire staff rushed out of the room, but the surgeon stoically stayed. She was, without question, destined to ensure this real-life drama played exactly as she for many scarred years had always imagined and dreamed during tormenting therapy sessions where she, from total terror, screamed.

# Barbara Eck Tosi

She instantly injected the man with Ritalin—an extremely large dose—that would painfully and permanently bring him out of his cozy comatose condition and finally force him to frighteningly come face-to-face with *her*—now busily preparing his perverted person to eternally erase.

The man was able to feverishly feel every shockingly sharp sensation that she, to him, was deliberately delivering with effervescent elation. To hardware secured to the surgical table, she tied his hands and feet. He belonged to *her* now, and her rightful revenge would be sublimely sweet.

*"You lowlife loser, lecherous louse, and sick, sadistic son of a bitch!* How ludicrously long I have waited to scratch this insanely insidious itch! You must now painfully pay for every vile thing you did and said to me years ago when you relentlessly ravished me and left me for dead.

"You pathologically penetrated my virgin body and left a horrifying smell that, after years of sterilizing showers, continues deep inside me to dwell. You wounded me with your wicked words and deeds so darkly depraved. Now your slime-slickened, salacious soul stands no chance of being saved.

"*Wanna play doctor, you wicked, worthless, wonder man wannabe?* Allow me to examine your abhorrently abscessed lower body cavity. Your gonorrhea-engorged genitals, glazed with a green, obscene disease, will disengage and fall to their deaths if you merely cough or sneeze.

"I will remove them with my serrated knife to prevent that from occurring. Now then, that was easy enough. Is that you I hear pleasantly purring? Don't worry that your mighty manhood will be at all negatively altered because you *never* were a man, and in manly things, you flagrantly faltered.

*"Say your quick and parting goodbyes to your disgustingly dirty thighs. I'm your* doctor now, *you felonious fraud,* and I seriously and strongly advise that you bid adieu to your appalling arms and hideously huge head, too, because they are the next particularly pathetic parts I plan to permanently undo.

"My surgical saw is tackling this task notably neatly and nicely. Now I'll affix the finishing touches as I slice through your torso thricely. You, *degenerate douchebag*, have made this day for me curiously charming. Your death now makes you unable to continue innocent women harming.

"I hope that *playing doctor* is something you have sincerely enjoyed because your *playtime* has ended, as I'm genuinely and proudly employed as a *real* doctor who, with the assistance of my sadistic saw and knife, has surgically removed every segment of you and silenced your shameful life.

"Never again will I allow myself to be vilely victimized and fall prey to that grotesquely ghastly game that soiled my soul in such a way that will perversely paralyze my psyche until death one day sets me free and guarantees that I will forever savor God's gift of sweet serenity.

*"Death will destroy you, perverted prick*, as you slowly waste away in your putrid place of perpetual pain and punishing permanent decay. *You are so dead, you deviant discombobulation of demon-dung-dipped debris.*

The

devil

and

you

are

damned

to

hell

for

an

endlessly

burning

eternity!"

# Hide-and-Freak

Deep inside an abandoned house that was more than considerably creepy, I opened my eyes wide to hide that I was still somewhat sleepy. My friends and I who lived beyond the bumpy banks of Crooked Creek gathered in the paint-peeling parlor for a fun-filled game of hide-and-seek.

Summertime was our sweet soul mate, and that is why we so often played this familiar game in this horrifying house where we for many hours stayed. Playing hide-and-seek stimulated our senses on the long, sun-drenched days and enticingly encouraged us to blissfully behave in carefree, childlike ways.

The hulking house hauntingly hinted at its hierarchy among hideous places where we could wholly hide our buoyant bodies and friendly faces until we were disappointingly discovered, and again, the game was played into the late and lazy afternoon when the summer sun began to fade.

The huge house had four strangely stacked stories that created a surreal sense of a larger-than-life, uneasy feeling of terrifyingly twisted and tense suspicious air that, when stirred by the sizzling and suffocating heat, forced each of us to frantically fidget and focus on our fiery feet.

Over the series of sun-soaked summers, we had seen nearly every space of this hunchbacked house that, from boredom, became our sole saving grace. Our melodious movements cleverly created a shocking and scintillating static that eerily electrified the four fearsome floors, which included the airless attic.

There was one particular place, however, that we deliberately never dared to enter because its reviled reputation resulted in us being beyond scared. The slightest suggestion of this spooky space spawned a soul-sucking alarm, so we avoided it because of our belief that it could hatch horrendous harm.

The cellar was that prohibitively petrifying place we feared so much that each of us promised its devilish doorknob never to approach or touch. A hundred years of being handled had left it wickedly worn and rusty, and the subsequent years of being undisturbed had left it diabolically dusty.

# Barbara Eck Tosi

Cellars caused our timid toes to curl because they were cold and creepy
and believed to be the dark dwelling places of every slimy, sleazy, and sleepy
vile, vicious vampire; wild, wretched witch; ghoulish goblin; and gossamer ghost
whose peculiar penchant for shuddersome cellars was what mortified us most.

A new game of hide-and-seek started, and I searched for the perfect place
where I could completely conceal myself and my fetchingly freckly face.
I was bewildered by the bothersome fact that I could not speedily spot
a nearby niche inside which I had a low risk of ever being caught.

The sleepy, sauntering sun with a solitary salute was shutting down,
and drooping groups of silver shadows signaled nightfall with their frown.
I was rapidly running out of spots where I could run and hurriedly hide,
even in this hideously humongous house, which was as tall as it was wide.

The time that I had to find a hiding place was rapidly running out too,
so I made an attempt to avoid the embarrassing "I found you."
If I were discovered before I was hidden, I would be forced to swallow
the litany of loud laughter that would, for the remainder of my life, follow.

The perilous path to the scary cellar was clearly the closest route
that I could with my ticking time find without being found out.
I timidly turned the rusty, dusty, dreadful, dangerous, deadly doorknob
and walked into the chill-filled cellar with my heart in a full-fledged throb.

I then quickly and quietly closed the cellar's severely splintered door
and frightfully followed the steep, squeaky stairs that led to the cellar floor.
Using the sparse light from a spider-webbed window as my solitary guide,
I seriously searched for a secluded spot to rapidly run and hurriedly hide.

I spotted something in a disturbingly dark corner that appeared to be
a perfect place where I could hide with absolute anonymity—
a restful retreat that would emphatically ensure I would never be found,
once I carefully climbed inside it without the slightest suggestion of sound.

# SCARY

It was a coffin that I had discovered, and inside its empty belly, I hid.
With only a trace of time remaining, I quickly lowered the lethal lid.
Now I simply needed to wait to be found or hear the familiar refrain
that would allow me to run upstairs and seek some sanity for my brain.

"Ollie, ollie, oxen free" were the wonderful words that so comforted me
as I struggled to lift the lid of the cockroach-crammed coffin to flee
and escape this miserable, musty, maleficent, and supernaturally scary cellar,
where I was deeply and deathly afraid, I would become a permanent dweller.

I attempted once again to lift the coffin's lid, but it remained solidly sealed.
As this hellish horror hovered, I hyperventilated, screamed, and squealed.
I heard my friends' voices as they left the hide-and-seek house and walked
outside where they amiably among their sparkling selves excitedly talked.

They said that I was most likely tired and with excessive heat so overridden
that I'd gone home—so they never knew I, in this house, was still hidden.
Their casual carefreeness about my well-being caused a chilling confusion
that made me think I was merely a horribly hideous hide-and-seek illusion.

My friends' lilting laughter lingered long after they winsomely walked away
while summer with sweet serenity inside its beautiful breezes did sway.
I shouted, pounded, prayed, and pleaded pathetically for their help,
but they were now much too far away to hear me thunderously yelp.

My family and friends believed that I had been egregiously eaten
by a wickedly ravenous animal or killed after being brutally beaten
by a treacherous troll traveling within the windy, whiny, wretched woods,
where my raw, fresh flesh was coldly sold to purchase select sundry goods.

The good-natured game of hide-and-seek was never again played—
at least not in that old, abandoned house where mixed memories weighed,
heavily inside the melancholy minds of my forlorn family and friends,
who viewed my untimely and disquieting death with unresolved loose ends.

I thought about serene sunny days, strawberry shortcake, and pink lemonade as I lay alone in the claustrophobic confines of the coffin's sadistic shade. In the cold, creepy cellar of this huge old house, dilapidated and decaying,

I

slowly

suffocated

inside

a

solidly

sealed

coffin

while

hide-and-seek

playing.

# Disenchanted Diners

She lacked a warm and welcoming relationship with her kitchen stove, which is why, on that yet eventless evening, her husband decisively drove to the debut of a fancy restaurant in this quintessentially quaint town, where the culinary word *cuisine* was the couple's most cherished noun.

Clean, crisp, white linen cloths covered the ritzy restaurant tables, and bottles of wine were divinely displayed with their prestigious labels, which artistically advertised the most revered and renowned varieties that filled the fine wine cellars of the world's wealthiest societies.

After the couple had the leather-bound menus studiously studied, the waiter, whose cheeks from unauthorized wine tasting were ruddied, took their dinner orders and then stumbled toward the noisy kitchen, where the banging of pots and pans pointed to some fractious friction.

After waiting a torturously tedious time for their dinners to arrive, the weary couple woefully wondered if their wobbly waiter was alive. When he finally appeared and robustly revealed his Riesling-red face, he served them frightfully foul food that was light-years beyond disgrace.

Their cold, raw, bloody sirloin steaks revealed obnoxious overhangs of thick, rubbery arteries scarier than a rattlesnake's fearsome fangs. The barely baked chicken touted terrifying tendons and bone slivers, causing the duo's duodenums to convulse from severe sphincter shivers.

Their raunchy, red-skinned potatoes, richly riddled with disgusting dirt, strikingly smelled like fresh cow manure mixed with a sizable squirt of a maniacal marinade made from pesticides and liquefied flies that did with an à la carte creepiness this concerned couple truly terrorize.

Their baby peas snoozed on cabbage leaves inescapably infested with fleas, and their soggy salad greens were blatantly black from a disabling disease. Their slime-smothered servings of fresh fruit were neither fruit nor fresh, and their forbidding, fermenting froth chilled the couple's fragile flesh.

# Barbara Eck Tosi

The half-baked loaf of week-old bread was menacingly moldy and hard, and the bitter butter that accompanied it resembled regurgitated lard. The characterless crackers were chipped from the noticeable nibbles of mice, whose telltale turds were miserably mixed with repulsively recycled rice.

The tap water inside their grimy goblets gave rise to a sickly storm that sadistically stalked a seismically stirred-up and super scary swarm of belligerent bumblebees that had all but lost their bothersome buzz as they fatally fell into the worrisome water, clad in black and yellow fuzz.

Alarmingly alive was the borderline blanched and brutally blistered lobster that lugubriously lumbered across their table like a drunken Mafia mobster, as it tried with dogged determination their fearful fingers to painfully pinch—a frantic antic that caused the crazed couple to fidget, freak, and flinch.

Their tea and coffee drowned inside bitingly bitter and muddy seas that caused a turbulent tsunami of gnarly grounds and lifeless leaves. The concrete clumps of caustic cane sugar relentlessly refused to dissolve, which clearly crippled the curdled cream's capability to completely revolve.

The couple, saturated with sickening shock from all the slop on their table, was catapulted into catatonic states that rendered them undeniably unable to unsee the petrifying picture of horror, they were now forced to face in the chilling confines of this corrupted and catastrophic culinary space.

The worthless waiter returned to the kitchen, where he safely remained conveniently incognito until he later reappeared with a red, wine-stained tray that was lusciously and life-threateningly laden with decadent desserts aptly accompanied by his compulsory and cautionary customer alerts.

The waiter furnished fair warning that these fabulous, first-class confections could lethally lead to life-altering addictions requiring insulin injections. He added that these sugar-saturated sweets were calamitously contagious and completely capable of causing a compulsiveness dangerously outrageous.

## SCARY

Before the waiter had a chance the deadly desserts to adequately describe,
the vigorously vehement, victimized couple began their defiant diatribe
by radically reprimanding him and doggedly demanding to see the chef,
as they vented with vocal veracity as if the wannabe waiter were deaf.

Within a short time, the chef made his awkwardly artificial appearance,
wearing cheap clothing he'd bought at a no-name, discount store clearance.
Below his dingy and dirty chef hat, his horrid head of hair could be seen,
dappled with dozens of dandruff flakes, disturbingly and overtly obscene.

His fatback face was filled with worrisome warts and bothersome boils,
and his exceptionally excessive ear hairs were curled like copper coils.
Significantly smelly sweat spilled forth from his pimply, putrid armpits
onto his slimy, snotty hands, which were smothered in zealous zits.

His horrendously hairy arms advertised aggravatingly abundant scabs
on which the concerned and cautious couple kept close and careful tabs
to ensure that the scabs, bordering on loose, did not inadvertently fall
onto their ill-fated table and create a very scary, scabby snow squall.

The chef's shameful shoes were slathered with gross gobs of grease
and dust and dirt and clumps of hair that did exponentially increase
the quickening, sickening sordidness of his septic and slovenly ways
and the frightfulness of his filthy food, which had seen much better days.

After the collapsed couple received emergency lifesaving resuscitation,
they vehemently vowed never again to repeat the deadly aggravation
that they encountered inside this raunchy restaurant ripe with revulsions
that came so close to killing them both with critical culinary convulsions.

They dramatically lost their desire to dine at restaurants, fancy or plain,
choosing, instead, to honor their TV trays to stay alive and sane.
They ate all their meals inside their home for the remainder of their lives,
fortified with food in supplement form acutely absent of sadistic surprise.

Never-endingly nauseated and nervously nearing a severe state of starvation, they attempted with absoluteness to annihilate the alarmingly awful agitation that numbed that nightmarish night and all the neurotic nights that followed, as they repulsively recollected the phantom food they had almost swallowed.

The culinarily challenged chef slipped and fell on the greasy kitchen floor. Upon standing, he slid straightaway through the open food freezer door, where he immediately impaled himself on a seriously sharp meat hook,

which

abruptly

ended

his

lousy

life

and

cursed

career

as

a

cook.

# Eyes on the Candy

My little sister and I went trick-or-treating in search of a huge sugar high one Halloween night beneath a thick, threatening, tactilely tenebrous sky. Disguised as human eyeballs, we confidently combed a classy neighborhood, darting from one decorated house to another like termites to weathered wood.

Our treat bags bulged from the bulky bounty of chubby chocolate bars that, after each of us ate just one, caused us to spin and see strange stars— not those seen in the spooky sky on dangerously dark and cloudless nights but those that signify self-induced sugar comas requiring religious *last rites*.

We were very protective of the precious bars, as if they came from Fort Knox, hiding them inside our bags with the strategic stealthiness of a fox. The bars promised that our food-of-the-gods fantasies would be fulfilled, provided we weren't by career candy snatchers cruelly captured and killed.

We gratefully grabbed the gobblicious goodies that were handed to us. They included heavenly homemade treats marked by a motherly fuss from a warm and whimsical woman who had the artsy-craftsy knack of fashioning a fabulous, festive, amazingly appealing Halloween snack.

Inside a soft swath of colorful cloth, she had placed each tempting treat. To emphatically ensure the delight of every trick-or-treater she would greet, she cinched the tops of the captivating cloths and then tied them tightly with royally resplendent ribbons that bound and beautified them brightly.

In various shades of the colors purple, orange, and bewitching black, the regal ribbons spectacularly stood out and caused us to stand back and admire this eye-blurring, creativity-stirring, trick-or-treat presentation that stoked and sharpened our senses with a haunting Halloween sensation.

We were, sometimes, surprised when quarters, nickels, pennies, and dimes were deposited into our ballooning bags to be set aside for rainy-day times. Occasionally, to our delirious delight, a crisp, conspicuous one-dollar bill would dangle from a generous outstretched hand, giving us a genuine thrill.

# Barbara Eck Tosi

For several hours we walked and talked and rang the deafening doorbells
of the profusely privileged people who populated the vibrant valleys and dells.
Our sagging sacks were so severely strained from sweet, sugar-saturated bliss,
we expected them to eventually explode with a big bang and horrendous hiss.

We suddenly stopped walking and stood to one side to seriously think about
how ludicrously late it was and how we could best get ourselves out
of this twisted trick-or-treat trap in which we were so tantalizingly tangled—
a fragile foothold fraught with bare trees and branches menacingly mangled.

In the distance upon a hellishly high hill, we spotted a lone, hulking house
that loomed over us as a curious cat looms over a cornered mouse.
We made the matter-of-fact decision that this house would be our last
one to visit in hopes of free candy; then we'd run back home very fast.

The huge house was disturbingly dark and sickly silent upon our arrival.
We felt the guarded gaze of evil eyes with intent heinously homicidal.
We thought this was a terrible trick to make us unquestionably believe
that a menacing monster lurking inside was warning us to quickly leave.

This confusing charade, however, coaxed our curiosity that much more
as we stepped onto the prickly pathway that led to a foreboding door.
We conjured up the courage of a shark-encircled, deep-sea squid.
Walk the perilous pathway to the door is what my little sister and I did.

We shivered as we rang the doorbell, which did not make a sound.
We were now more than slightly scared, but we refused to turn around.
To this house with its harbinger of candy, we were wholly committed.
Nothing and no one could cause it from our intended itinerary to be omitted.

When not a soul appeared at the front door, our spirited selves to greet
with chocolate candy bars, shiny coins, or a handsome homemade treat,
we fearfully turned the gnarly knob on the unexpectedly unlocked door,
and anxiously anticipating a cache of candy, walked onto a wooden floor.

# SCARY

With horror on a scale of the scariest and most spine-splintering kind,
we faced a horrifying *Halloween trick* that rendered us permanently blind.
A feral fiend's ferocious focus on freakish, fateful, forbidding misfortunes
caused our bowels and bladders to experience extremely emergent eruptions.

A wretched witch with lethally long fingernails ominously outstretched
painfully poked out our eyes and then feverishly and fanatically fetched
our heavy Halloween treat bags and then proceeded to pick out and eat
all of the candy contained inside as blood rushed to our petrified feet.

Without our excruciatingly extracted eyeballs, we still desperately tried
to discover in the devilish darkness a way to get ourselves safely outside.
Despite the fact we had no eyes and were steeping in shocked states of mind,
we miraculously managed the wicked witch's bolted back door to find.

How we arrived home to tell the terrible tale remains an unsolved mystery.
To prevent you from ever repeating our horrifically horrible Halloween history,
we must warn you never to go near that haunted house on Halloween night,

because

if

you

do

you

too,

might

lose

all

of

your

candy

and

your

sight.

# The Proctor

It happened following the conclusion of the stellar student's final exam, for which she many dedicated days and wearying weeks did cram. The large classroom was considerably cramped as every chair was filled. Although the room was hideously hot, the eerie air was curiously chilled.

She sat predictably at her desired desk located last in the far end row, in the back of the room where she had comfortably come to know the stable safety, perpetual protection, and unfettered freedom that she most necessarily needed to emphatically ensure her sweet sense of serenity.

Beneath the black, boxy chalkboard appeared the overweight proctor's desk, which handsomely handcrafted from hickory wood was quite picturesque. At the perfectly placed picturesque desk, the portly proctor promptly sat. He was a fiercely foreboding figure who was balder than a hairless cat.

A short time after he sat down, the proctor issued his cold command, and every single scared-to-death student placed a pencil in one hand. As soon as the proctor started the tensely ticking, terrifying timer, the exam began, as did the pressure felt by each academic climber.

The claustrophobic class tackled the torturous test that shiveringly stared at their bruised brains that drained from study were then dauntingly dared with only accurate answers all the quirky questions to frantically feed— a strategy sure to scholastically ensure that those students would succeed.

She picked up her pointed pencil and, with a calm and confident heart, glanced at the final exam and disturbingly displayed a surreal, scary start. The pudgy proctor walked past her desk and staunchly and sadistically stood directly and deliberately behind her, much like a stone statue would.

It was overtly obvious to the student that he had no inclination or intention to move to a distinctly different location, and she lacked the courage to mention to him that her beautiful, brilliant brain had become permanently paralyzed the second he shockingly stood behind her, and he had her traumatized.

## Barbara Eck Tosi

The very last seat in the far end row could no longer at any time provide the student's security, once so treasured, now sentenced to forever hide. An unprecedented urgency made her feel unsafe and undeniably unprotected because her every thought to the perilous proctor had been direly deflected.

She sat motionless in her chilly chair and was utterly unable to think. Her glassy, glazed, and empty eyes were firmly fixed and ceased to blink. Her breathtaking brain had been sadly short-circuited, and this painful pause forced the disturbing display of her emotionally epic and fatal flaws.

The proctor stood behind the student's desk for the duration of the exam, cruelly killing her concentration as a wicked wolf kills a helpless lamb. Her permeating panic pulsated, and her scholarly spark sharply sank. When the exam time finally came to an end, her paper remained blank.

Before the permanently pathetic proctor to his hickory desk returned, she savagely stabbed him with her pointed pencil because he had earned the failing and fatal *grade of death* for being the radically ridiculous reason

she

failed

this

final

exam

during

her

scholastically

stellar

season.

# Shepherd's Pie

The famished sheep farmer devoured his devilishly divine shepherd's pie.
Fresh meat and garden vegetables beneath its mashed potatoes did lie.
Savory gravy gravitated toward the mixed garden greens and meat
as the sheep farmer at his kitchen table took a most anxious seat.

His shoddy, shabby shoes were heinously holey, mud-covered, and worn,
and his thoroughly threadbare trousers were disgustingly dirty and torn.
His shameful shirt was substantially stained from the blood of sheep
that, from being shorn too close to the bone, had bled from cuts deathly deep.

The sheep farmer watched the shepherd through the broken glass pane
of his weathered window now powerfully pelted with relentless rain,
which catapulted carelessly and ceaselessly off the savagely splintered sill
with the frightening ferocity of a psychotic with a propensity to kill.

For years the sheepish shepherd had been in the sheep farmer's employ,
dating back to when the shepherd was barely a grown-up boy.
In exchange for his work, a tiny cottage and small stipend it was decided
would, in addition to hot, wholesome suppers, be for him duly provided.

The stalwart shepherd and his dedicated dogs spent their days in the fields
herding the shifting sheep that would produce the woolen yields
that allowed the sheep farmer, his wife, and the shy shepherd to survive
a livelihood that often challenged their ability to live and thrive.

The sheep farmer's wife had recently died, leaving him futilely forlorn.
She was buried behind the barn, where the sheep were twice-yearly shorn.
From a singular sheep-shearing snafu, she had painfully and tragically died.
Since that time, the farmer had the shearing with considerable caution eyed.

Untethered by the ridiculous routine rituals of personal hygiene,
he blatantly became a septic specimen, unsettlingly smelly and obscene.
His fixated failure to bathe and shave and wash his long, lice-laden hair
created a sickening stench that severely stung the surrounding air.

## Barbara Eck Tosi

His moldy bread swiftly surrendered inside his serving of shepherd's pie,
greedily grabbing the greasy gravy that was seasoned with salt and a fly.
The pie was heartily heaped with fresh meat from the kill of the day
and soon soiled the tattered tablecloth with its gobs of gravy gone astray.

The sheep farmer wiped his messy mouth on his frightfully filthy shirt
and blew his seriously snot-filled nose with the old kitchen table's skirt.
With his monstrous mouth, he emptied dark beer from his stoneware stein
and anxiously anticipated more as if it flowed freely from the river Rhine.

As the clock insanely ticked and tocked and sharpened its chilling chime,
the deliriously drunk farmer passed out cold in a shockingly short time,
awaking later in the vomit he'd wretched during his alcoholic binge
that coated him in cold, creamy chunks that caused him to cuss and cringe.

The shepherd's long, tedious day tending sheep was usually over by ten
o'clock when the inky black, star-scattered sky summons hungry men,
who scarf down their late-night suppers until they feel fully fed
and then polish off pints of sleep-inducing beer that force them into bed.

The shepherd should have, hours earlier, anxiously arrived at the door
of the sheep farmer's house for his well-deserved hot supper to implore.
The farmer stepped out into the cold and called the shepherd's name,
but after waiting and receiving no response, back inside, he quickly came.

Still in a spirited stupor, he thought about the events of the unfolding day
and remembered something startling he found deep inside a bale of hay.
It was a small wooden box that his late wife had loved and cherished,
and inside it was a love letter she had received before she perished.

The letter had been written by the shepherd who prolifically proclaimed
his pure and lasting love for her—a love of which he was unashamed.
Next to the letter, a gold locket with his initials symbolically revealed
the enduring love the two soul mates had shared with hearts forever sealed.

## SCARY

The sheep farmer beheld his bloody knife and then readily remembered that he had, earlier that day, the shepherd killed and totally dismembered. He had buried him behind the barn beside his unfaithful and ungrateful wife, but not before removing pieces of him with the blade of his razor-sharp knife.

He had placed the prized pieces of the shepherd into his kitchen sink, where they had marinated in a bath of beer so they would not begin to stink. These moist, meaty morsels for his midday meal did sumptuously supply

the

phenomenally

fresh

and

fertile

flesh

for

his

special

shepherd's

pie.

# A Hand and a Leg

Her only hand was disturbingly deformed—madly misshapen and divided into several segmented sections, unusually unique and ludicrously lopsided. Her disfigured digits were dictated by dastardly dents and a curious crimp that not only resembled but convincingly copycatted a curly cocktail shrimp.

Her vulgar veins were as vulnerable as a suddenly surfacing submarine and brazenly bulged above her scaly skin to a rhythm overtly obscene. Her knobby and knotted knuckles buckled beneath behemoth bumps that could easily be mistaken for a cluster of killer whale humps.

Her skin's shell-shocked sheath showed significant signs of bruisings whose colors mimicked those of a rainbow ripe with odiferous oozings. The slippery, slithering, shuddersome slime that from the oozings arose was garishly green and hellishly yellow, like pus residing inside a nose.

But a gorgeous, glistening, translucent trail she did liberally leave behind when she slid over the soft sand's surface as a slug that one would find caressing a cobblestone path that placidly punctuated a wildflower glen whose protective pines provided shelter for each woodland rabbit and wren.

Her heavy heart was bleakly bleeding, and her stiff legs felt like lead as she consistently continued with one hand to awkwardly amble ahead. Her faithful friends were the sublimely sweet and salty sea creatures that viewed her enchanting eccentricities as endearingly flattering features.

This one-handed woman wistfully wondered if she would someday wed or be forced to miserably marinate in her mucousy misfortune instead. Heartbroken by having only one hand, she slowed her shimmering pace and resigned herself to the fatalistic future she was forlornly forced to face.

The limitless liquids that leaked from her labyrinth of liberal lumps; the disgusting, disfigured digits with their battalion of barbaric bumps; and the mystifying missing hand did not, for a moment, scare or deter, the heavenly heartthrob who hovered nearby and hoped to marry her.

The sweet souls seemed shockingly similar as they stood side by side against the background of singing seagulls and the salty, sultry tide. The motivated man with his only leg solidly situated inside the sand

breathlessly

begged

the

beautiful

woman

for

her

one

and

only

hand.

# Above and Beyond

With a preponderance of pampered plants, her cluttered cottage was filled, until they were, by her compulsive kindness, carelessly and quickly killed. Their deaths resulted from the well-meaning woman's overt overcaring, which collided with her tenacious tendency to be overly overbearing.

This counterintuitive combination sorely sabotaged her every goal and helplessly held her hostage inside a big, bitter, beleaguered bowl of her chronically challenged, constantly cursed, and copious creative juices, which were strangled by her oddly obtrusive, obsessive-compulsive nooses.

Now painfully and pitifully plantless, she looked for alternative avenues where she could actualize her artistic abilities without ever having to lose the prized products of her patent perfection, so without further looking, she tenaciously tackled the tasty task of recipe-inspired baking and cooking.

With common, convenient culinary contraptions and a famous cookbook, she eagerly embraced this exciting enterprise that, by hook or by crook, would enable her to enjoy the syndrome of self-centered saturation that was the quintessential hallmark of her task-obsessed infatuation.

The cookbook's instructions, with no exceptions, were completely clear so that klutzy cooks and bungling bakers would not have to face the fear of creating culinary catastrophes that certainly had no conceivable place on dining room tables dramatically dressed in delightful Dresden lace.

Indescribably immersed in her new homey hobby, she sat on her rocker, restlessly rifling through relentless recipes in her reclusive Betty Crocker cookbook within whose prophetic pages lay the glimmering golden key that would officially open the flour-dusted door to her culinary longevity.

As she perused random recipes, she stumbled upon meatloaf instructions, which, in time, would positively prove to have irreversible repercussions. But at this pivotal point in this suspenseful story, solely suffice it to say, to the summit of Meatloaf Mountain, she was well on her culinary way!

Betty's recipe required one pound of a bona fide butcher's ground beef, but the woman possessed the strong, steadfast, albeit scary, belief that, if she, to make this memorable meatloaf, used twenty pounds instead, it would guarantee that her faithful family would be especially well-fed.

The woman omitted the option of adding ground pork and ground veal due to her ample addition of ground beef, which did make her feel that she, of this renowned recipe, was in complete creative control, and she alone would tweak the ingredients to suit her spunky soul.

One beaten egg and assorted amounts of minced onion, pepper, and salt were among the culinary coconspirators contained in Betty's vault. True to her nature, the woman added twenty eggs and twenty onions—Vidalias, which she believed would be beneficial for her bunions.

Into the buxom, beefed-up bowl, she poured a sizable slew of salt—exactly twenty pounds of it because it would surely not be *her* fault if the meatloaf was not salty enough for her entire family to please. To add some sass, she threw in twenty pounds of curry and celery seeds.

Twenty pounds of pungent pepper to this massive mound she added next, as she, seismically sneezing, struggled to decipher the meaty text of the revered recipe from her new, best buddy, Betty Crocker, whose cookbook creepily cornered her like an escaped psychotic stalker.

She marveled that this mighty meatloaf, when she declared it was done, would eclipse every epicurean edible that was ever eaten by anyone. Her penchant for perfection persisted as she pondered the recipe page, reassuring herself that she, like Betty, would be a celebrated culinary sage.

Betty's recipe called for one cup of dry breadcrumbs or bread cubes, but because the *Betty Crocker wannabe* wished not the pressure to choose, she added both the breadcrumbs and bread cubes to the mixture of meat—twenty pounds of each that did all the other ingredients disastrously greet.

# SCARY

At this point in the production, even her biggest bowls were too small. There was woefully not a wee whit of wiggle room available at all in which to add and mix the mounting multitude of other tasty things that a consummate and charismatic cook congenially to the table brings.

The meaty monster was so massive that it, mandatorily, in the bathtub sat because the bathtub was quite clearly the only plausible place that the woman could aggressively attempt to completely combine and mix this confusing concoction that not even Betty Crocker herself could fix.

Intoxicated by indications that the insidious ingredients were well mixed, the woman paused, caught her breath, and then appeared to be transfixed—first with dazed amazement at what she had quite craftily created, and then with total terror, once her dazed amazement had abruptly abated.

She realized that she needed to transfer this utterly unmanageable mixture to her kitchen and into her oven, which was notably not a large fixture. Her cramped kitchen now seemed as if it were a million miles away from the barely big enough bathtub wherein the miserable meatloaf lay.

Before the worried woman could this tense and tedious transfer initiate, she was fitfully forced over her oven's ill-equipped interior to officiate. She precisely knew how she must rearrange the inside of her oven so it would allow the meatloaf to gain its grand entrance and comfortably fit.

She removed all the metal oven racks with the mere exception of one in hopes of garnering sufficient space to adequately hold this megaton of maniacal meat that she inside her seriously snug stove would pile and then permit to bake undisturbed for a very, very, very long while.

She was unquestionably sure that her oven was now perfectly prepared to welcome the massive mound of meat that at her very scarily stared. Unequivocally crystal clear was the next necessary step she must take: remove the raw meat from the bathtub and place it into the oven to bake.

The terribly tiresome trips she trekked from the bathtub to the oven most certainly exceeded the numbing number of a torturous twenty dozen. As she felt the persistent pain of newly budding and bothersome bunions, she was thankful that her meatloaf contained ample amounts of Vidalia onions.

As the determined woman carefully attempted to close the tiny oven door, prodigious pieces of raw meatloaf dangerously dropped to the kitchen floor. It was blatantly beyond obvious that her little oven could not contain her masterpiece, which ubiquitously unraveled into unrelenting meaty rain.

This unexpected meat storm did not at all this wonder woman deter, as she was utterly, unabashedly, undeniably, overtly, and obsessively sure that her mystifyingly marvelous meatloaf in a short, sweet time would be recorded as *The Mother of All Meatloaves* in the annals of culinary history.

The oven temperature that would the beloved Betty Crocker aptly appease was a perfect, preapproved, and predestined 350 degrees. Betty advised that the meatloaf be baked for one and a half hours, after which time it could be served on fine china with hand-painted flowers.

The woman's intuition was outlandishly *outside-the-cookbook* based. She believed her masterful meatloaf would undoubtedly much better taste if she, bravely, from the very beginning, set the oven dial to a brazen broil, so the raw meat inside the very small oven would not prematurely spoil.

For three disheartening days, she held a constant vigil over the stove while her family, ordered by her to eat out, to local restaurants drove. They were now married to memories of the restaurants' meatloaf dinners and, consequently, felt the collective guilt of the world's worst sinners.

The family was astutely and acutely aware that the woman's sense of worth was irreversibly dependent upon her beloved meatloaf's successful birth. They also knew it was incredulously idiotic to automatically assume that her meatloaf would come close to full term inside the oven's womb.

## SCARY

After four fretful days in the tiny oven, the meatloaf, both burnt and raw, continued at the woman's collapsing confidence to aggravatingly gnaw. But her love for this, her first meatloaf, made her utilize her time with an increasingly insane intensity that boldly bordered on cold crime.

After five frustrating days in the oven, the miserable meatloaf finally died. The woman reluctantly turned off its life support as she copiously cried. A spicy specimen that survived her overly ambitious and cursed creation appeared as a butchered beef-tartare-and-badly-burnt-jerky combination.

She remained indefatigably undefeated, though, as she did readily realize that an ill-begotten meatloaf would never jeopardize her timeless ties to the considerably creative world that welcomed her passion and pizazz that cleverly concealed her OCD, divinely dolloped with a dab of jazz.

The well-meaning woman wisely decided to throw her worn apron away. Never again did she her now-infamous Betty Crocker cookbook display. Doggedly determined and fearlessly focused, she prepared to face her fate

the

very

next

day,

when

she,

every
inch
of
her
house,
would
redecorate.

# Sinfully Spectacular Sensations

Loaded, locked, and lifeless inside their vaults of stark solid steel, the clandestine corpses were consumed by their lack of sensation to feel. The caustic coldness licked their stiffness with its terrifying tongue and fixated its frightful frigidness above them where it hovered and hung.

How these humans met their deaths does not at this juncture matter. Of importance is that prime parts of them would soon become the batter inside the mild-mannered medical examiner's overzealous food blender and then be transformed into creative concoctions for the bakery vendor.

Sacks of sugar and sundry secret surprises bettered every blessed batch whose amazingly appetizing appeal no other confectioners could match. The medical examiner's trailblazing techniques fed the fabulous flavor and transformed it into flawless fineness that even fickle folks did savor.

The madly methodical medical examiner remained rambunctiously ready to proceed with the perfected process that provided him with a steady supplemental income, rewarding recognition, and fitting folk hero fame due to this colossal collection of confections celebrating his family name.

With an anxious ax, he hastily hacked off each captive corpse's head and its hands, feet, arms, and legs, all of which blissfully bled. Artfully arranged in an attic, the assorted appendages avoided attention. After a bonus butchering blitz, they were bound for bakery perfection.

The medical examiner created captivating cakes and prize-winning pies, and splendid specialty breads and buns, because he did smartly, surmise that *more* is blatantly better than less and *better* significantly more sells the sublime, sugary, and savory specimens that spawn cerebral cell swells.

The hacked-off heads and oodles of organs were thrice toasted and ground into a premiere, pearlized powder, whose delicate dust would be found on the tempting tops of braided breads and bodaciously behemoth buns that awaited the customers' longing lips and tips of their tantalized tongues.

The taste bud-tempting torsos were quartered and pounded perfectly flat and daintily dropped into a blistering, boiling, and volcanically virile vat of gorgeous, golden grease that rendered them crispy, crunchy, and brown, in perfection-permeated preparation for their tenacious travel into town.

The earlier extracted eyeballs were injected with scrumptious sweet cream— the kind found inside the doughnuts that cause sugar addicts to scream. The enchanting eyeballs secured the stares of the seasoned shoppers, who thought they were merely playful props posing as store showstoppers.

Every drib and every drab of every dead body was deliciously used— a fact that enabled the eager examiner to always be astonishingly amused, as one monumentally meaningful motto he did honorably and heartily heed. Here is that motto for you to read: "'Waste not, want not' does the deed!"

The austere autopsy room, characteristically cold and hurtfully heartbreaking, was satisfyingly saturated with the smells of sweet and savory things baking. After excitedly exiting the oven, they would completely cool on rigid racks and then be packaged as meal companions and sensational, satisfying snacks.

Copious quantities of charming cakes and a plethora of palate-pleasing pies would be decoratively displayed with the double-dreamy, cream-filled eyes, a stellar selection of beautiful buns, and a bounty of bewitching breads, dusted with the pearlescent powder from pulverized organs and heads.

This potpourri of popular pastries and breads signaled the signature success of this self-made man who, the contents of his confections, would never confess. Prevalently positioned on every prized package was the name of his creations:

"Dr.

Rottingbod's

Sweet,

Savory,

and

Sinfully

Spectacular

Sensations!"

# The Fat Cat Door

As the old woman inside her colorful cottage garden dizzily danced, she, mesmerized by its boundless beauty, became electrifyingly entranced. Her magical movements stirred the spirits of her fragrant, fragile flowers that were saturated with the sacredness of spring's soft, soulful showers.

The rain's gentle genuflection soothed the sprawling swath of lazy land that lay lusciously and luxuriously beneath a perfect Prussian blue band of silky sky whose light brightened the dense thicket of tangled trees, within which woodland life slumbered inside a blissful, beckoning breeze.

The old woman was irreversibly immersed in her compulsive clipping of the dead debris from her famished flowers, which were serenely sipping the rainwater that so willingly and lovingly their thirsty souls did nourish with the refreshment that enabled them to gregariously grow and flourish.

The woman exuded pure inner peace as she silently and swiftly snipped and pulled the unwieldy weeds that with delicious drops of water dripped. Her earthly heaven hovered with holiness high above her humble being, as she, for now, enjoyed the serenity of God's gentle gardens seeing.

She gracefully gathered the perturbing pile of unruly, unwanted weeds and paused to ponder how perfectly her godly garden satisfied her needs. The time and endless energy she, in its welfare, did earnestly invest, coupled with nature's nurturing, ensured it always looked its best.

She persistently pampered the fair flowers so they would bud and bloom and not prematurely and permanently enter their inevitable earthly tomb. The autumnal frost with its bitterly biting and cruelly caustic chill would ultimately her beloved bevy of beauties brutally and abruptly kill.

As the woman dutifully deadheaded her bee balm, buttercups, and lilies, she daftly developed and drolly displayed a curious case of *the sillies*, which launched her lively laughter and desire to delightfully dance again while irresistibly intoxicated by Mother Nature's zigzagging Zen.

Obviously oblivious to everything existing outside her floral world, she never noticed the malevolent movements that had been eerily unfurled by the parish pastor who, without invitation, walked her cobblestone path to devilishly deliver a self-absorbed sermon centered on simple math.

The woman had ceased contributing to the collection plate at her church during Sunday services when the congregants were left in the lurch because the pastor failed to publicly announce the exact total amount of money received as he used it to pad his personal bank account.

Pastor Rennis was a man who was frightfully fat, fake, and foul-spoken and had each of God's holy commandments brazenly and brainlessly broken several times over but continued to possess the ugly and ungodly gall that bolstered his belief that he, not his flock, stood sinless, saintly, and tall.

The shady pastor sneakily stepped up to the cottage's sunny front door, rudely ripe and ready some money from the woman to impolitely implore. He planned to convince her that commencing her weekly cash donations would readily result in the congregation's congratulatory standing ovations.

He would blither about beefing up *the bread* she placed in the collection plate, which would guarantee her entrance to heaven through God's golden gate. If truth be told, it would lavishly line the predatory pastor's piggish pockets and bring about a bizarre bulging of his evil eyes and eroding eye sockets.

The old woman owned a distinctively dapper and deeply devoted house cat that was sublimely soft, genuinely gentle, and forbiddingly freakishly fat. She allowed her cat to come and go whenever he purringly pleased by opening and closing her front entry door to keep him amply appeased.

She had arranged for a *fat cat door* in her cottage kitchen to be installed to prevent her cat companion from being aggravated, attacked, and mauled by the wretchedly wicked wildlife that so stealthily and sinisterly stalked anything and everything that within the wildly winding woodland walked.

# SCARY

Her fat cat fancied the *fat cat door* that for him had been expressly made. The cat was now able during every season, in both sunshine and shade, to effortlessly exit and enter the cottage without ever becoming stuck and converted to a coveted covered dish at a wicked, wildlife potluck.

Upon the woman's welcoming door, Pastor Rennis obnoxiously knocked. His nasty knock went unanswered, so he opened the door and walked inside, where, with horror, he witnessed a sick and shocking sight—an assemblage of appetite-accelerated animals prepared with him to fight.

Four behemoth, blood-lusty beasts boldly badgered the petrified pastor. Their jutting jaws and tensely tapping teeth told the tale that *faster* was the speed at which they would spring upon this sinister sinner, and *torn apart* was the way his flesh would be presented for their dinner.

A wretched wolf with malignant mange manifested his malicious teeth as his grim, glazed, gelatinous eyes glared at the pastor from underneath the kitchen table where the wound-up wolf watched his shaking sheep and wildly waited for the mortal moment upon him to lethally leap.

A beastly, brazen, boisterous, bulky, and brutally barbaric boar caused the pastor's asphyxiating anxiety to significantly soar. A wry red fox, revoltingly rabid, did relish in revealingly wearing his sickly saliva, which he with the panicked pastor would be sharing.

A brawny, belligerent, bloodthirsty, and breathless backwoods bear cast his fearsome, fiendish, ferocious, famished, and fateful stare upon the tensely twitching body of this undeniably unholy man, who pleadingly prayed to God for a ready-and-waiting getaway van.

These baneful, bug-eyed beasts toward the paralyzed pastor were rushing. Their truculent teeth tore through his torso, and blood began gushing. Like perturbed piranhas, they pursued the panting pastor until they tasted him and then ate every fleshy fiber that was, with his bad blood, basted.

They licked clean his dripping bones and maintained the extremely mean look of angry, aggressive attackers whose hunger for humans was keen. They left behind no forensic evidence or tantalizing telltale trace that something horrifically horrid here had moments before taken place.

The mad menagerie of murderous monsters fled in a formidable flurry by way of the fat cat door, which they had earlier entered in a hurry. The pathetic Pastor Rennis, off the global grid, had deservedly disappeared into the bulging bellies of beasts that he for his whole life had feared.

Mothering her mystical flowers had left the old woman insanely inspired, as well as horrendously hungry, terribly thirsty, and terrifically tired. From her plethora of posies, she picked a particularly pleasing bouquet that she, once inside, would in her cottage kitchen divinely display.

She entered her quaint cottage, which was compellingly clean and neat, and made her way to the cozy kitchen where she planned to take a seat on her white wicker rocker beside the wide-eyed window to rest her beleaguered bones, maladjusted muscles, and clearly congested chest.

She artfully arranged her freshly fetched flowers in a vintage violet vase and placed it on her kitchen table atop a long-lived, light lavender lace doily that she had craftily crocheted during her celebrated salad days and for its unusual, intricate design had rightfully received much praise.

The woman eventually inquired as to the whereabouts of Pastor Rennis, as did the woodland villagers, who had long deemed him a major menace, to the very sanctity of their cherished church and committed congregation and viewed his disappearance as a certain cause for Christian celebration.

A new pastor soon took charge and monitored the makeover of the mess that had, for much too long, punished the parishioners with paralyzing stress. He masterfully managed Pastor Rennis' missteps to mindfully mend. After that, with religious regularity, the woman did Sunday services attend.

## SCARY

She conscientiously collected her coins and cash and placed them into the weekly offering plate, which would in God's time amazingly accrue, the mountain of money required to fund the everlasting implementation of choice, church projects sure to guarantee the congregation's salvation.

Pastor Rennis had long been in the woodland beasts' dirty dung discarded and washed away by forest rains that with great reverence were regarded. On Sunday mornings, the church members converge and listen with intent,

to

Pastor

Goodman,

who

all

believe

was

by

their

holy

God

heaven-sent.

# Amazing Glaze

The kitchen cupboards were painted a serene shade of winter white beneath a gorgeous glacier-white glaze that mimicked a full moon's light. The cupboards were artfully adorned with arctic-white porcelain knobs that resembled those seen on the coveted cupboards of society snobs.

The kitchen's walls and coffered ceiling were covered in wisteria-white paint and glaze that resplendently reflected the beautifully bright white light that, in the early morning hours, engendered extraordinarily enchanting hues, more pleasing than those a professional decorator could conceivably choose.

An oleander-white cotton cloth covered the old, wooden kitchen table, upon which sprawled a sweet, soft white cat that was effortlessly able to deliciously devote its narcissistic nine lives to napping the hours away against the brilliant and breathtaking backdrop of this avalanche-white array.

In clearly confusing contrast to this perfect, pristine, and poetic palate stood a disturbingly dark, hellishly heavy, wickedly worn wooden mallet. From its place in the adjoining den, it ghoulishly glared at the kitchen and scarily showed its superiority as a ready reactor to fractious friction.

The mallet leaned against a mantel that writhed and worrisomely waned due to the weight of witnessing something that had been patently pained by insanely invasive and inexplicably inescapable clusters of clotted cold that heinously haunted the hideous den with their horrendously heavy hold.

The old woman kept her biscuits and tea in a place easy for her to inspect so that when her supply of either dwindled, she could quickly this fact detect. To ensure that she, her biscuits, and tea could always congregate face-to-face, she stored them in her narcissus-white cupboard, which was the perfect place.

Draped in darkness near the narcissus-white cupboard was an identical one, the inside of which, for over a century, had never seen the face of the sun. A hundred years' worth of dreary dust decorated its eerily ethereal exterior, making the woman's biscuit-and-tea cupboard seem superlatively superior.

## Barbara Eck Tosi

Peculiar paint and a ghoulish glaze had penetrated and permanently sealed this cobwebbed copycat cupboard that with sordid savageness squealed, as if it had suffered severely and surreally from a punishing, paralyzing pain, due to an annihilating absence of air during its heinous, hundred-year reign.

The woman was helplessly hampered by being hereditarily hard of hearing, and that is why she never heard the scary, sickly, and sustained searing, of something sinister that inside the cupboard supernaturally screamed and with the weird, warped whines of evil entrapment very tellingly teamed.

The woman sought some supplementary space to keep her tea and confections. Her mind explored satisfactory solutions that took her in different directions. When she eyed the cobwebbed copycat cupboard, she quickly came to realize that it was positively the perfect place to house her surplus supplies.

No one, but she, was there to break the copycat cupboard's stymied seal, so, using her innately innovative ingenuity and surprising strength and zeal, she created a promising plan of action that would enable her to securely store her backup supply of biscuits and tea behind the sealed cupboard door.

She picked up the worn wooden mallet and used it to strike the knob— an award-worthy action that simultaneously started and finished the job of breathtakingly breaking the century-old seal of wicked white paint and glaze that had held the cupboard contents captive for many millions of days.

The massive mallet was maliciously ripped from the woman's helpless hands, and her white-hair-covered head was pounded until lethally large bands of her blood displayed themselves on the wretchedly white, weeping walls, that now, gushing with rushing blood, resembled a red Niagara Falls.

Monopolizing the murderous mallet was a mercilessly menacing, young girl. Clad in clothing from a bygone era, she possessed hair with a transfixing twirl. Her fiendish eyes were forebodingly fixated on the functionless and fractionated old woman, who, after enduring more mallet misery, was overtly obliterated.

## SCARY

"I've been confined in this claustrophobic cupboard for over a hundred years," the ghoulish girl belligerently bellowed as her eyes swelled with angry tears. "My monster of a mother as painful punishment placed me in here when I, inside my little brother's devil's food cake, hid a demonstrably dead horsefly.

"'You're a very, very, *very* bad girl, so in the cupboard, you now must go,' my mother scolded, 'and not one solitary soul on this earth will ever know, because your beautifully behaved brother and I will forever and beyond be in a safe and secret space that you, demon daughter, will sadly never see.'

"And you, you old worthless woman, with your empty ears never heard my chronic cries and ceaseless screams, as it never once to you occurred, to unseal and reveal what has long waited inside this cursed cupboard door,

until

now,

when

I'm

finally

free,

and

you're

deservedly

dead

on

the

floor!"

# Piece of Mind

Her wretchedly warped world unwound into a nothingness, blackish gray.
Her lifeless life listlessly languished in dark, desolate, desperate disarray.
She silently prayed for an eternal end to the unbearable and unrelenting pain
that bombarded her barely-there body and soul and made her quite insane.

Her insidious insanity, like a beaver chewing on splintered river wood,
gnawed incessantly at her unsettledness and unflinchingly stood
in the confused center of her uneasy essence, which forced her to retreat
into the corners where scary spiders and their creepy cobwebs meet.

She screamingly sought the soothing serenity of her silent, soulful place,
where she could shed her severely scarred skin and, finally, freely face
the twisted, tortured thoughts and viciously venomous vitriolic voices
that fatally forced her to mindlessly make irrational and irreversible choices.

Her cherished cottage conveyed a calmness consistent with cathartic healing
and discouraged her dangerously destructive demons from summarily stealing,
the mellow moments, silent solitude, and poetically pure pieces of peace
that only in this most sacred space could discover their most sweet release.

She arrived in time to savor the sunshine, so brilliantly bright and blinding,
hoping for the eerily elusive possibility of perfect *peace of mind* finding.
The warm woodland winds whisked away her weariness as she quietly slept
until the dreaded darkness over her quilt-covered body cryptically crept.

The shock-sickened sky saturated the sinister scene that stared and stood,
scarily above the quickly thickening thicket of warped, weathered wood.
Her pursuit of peace of mind had been to the chaotic, careening cosmos sent
as her cozy, cherished cottage was abhorrently attacked and brutally bent.

Pensive pines, plainly possessed by phantoms of this feral forest's dead,
thrust their tortured, traumatized trunks onto her torso, which balefully bled.
Wicked wolves viciously ripped apart her limbs and then wantonly wallowed,
in her phenomenally fresh flesh, which they savagely and sinfully swallowed.

Her wretchedly warped world unwound into a nothingness, blackish gray.
Her lifeless life listlessly languished in dark, desolate, desperate disarray.
She had soulfully sought some peace of mind in this once protected place.

Pieces

of

her

mind

now

fed

the

wolves

that

left

no

tell-tale

trace.

# The Next-Door Neighbor

Victoria's wealthy father had bequeathed her a seriously substantial sum of money, that upon its receipt, had rendered her speechless and numb. With her impressive inheritance, she purchased a vintage Victorian home with sprawling spaces that secured her safe sanctuaries in which to roam.

Her next-door neighbor was a single gentleman, from what she had been told. He was a brilliant businessman whose savvy solvency stemmed from the bold and venerable ventures, which he vivaciously and victoriously directed, when his moneymaking mind was not, by all beautiful women, deflected.

Victoria was not aware that his only true love had most tragically died, and that since that unbelievably unbearable time, the unsettled man had tried to discover someone strikingly special who came the very closest to being, the wonderful woman he wept for daily and woefully missed seeing.

His name was Albert, and he steadfastly stood at the elegant entry door of Victoria's Victorian villa soon after she returned from the grocery store. His knocking drew her out of the pantry that she was methodically stocking and to her stately stained-glass door, through which she started talking.

Through the glass, she glimpsed a definitively dapper, dark-haired stranger, asked him who he was, what he wanted, and decisively detected danger. She kept her entry door locked and bolted, until which time he did explain that he was her next-door neighbor and not someone inarguably insane.

His primary purpose, he purported, was to meet and warmly welcome her to her new neighborhood, which, he noted, had a most amazing allure. After he unmasked his mouth-watering muffins, she opened her door wide and politely invited her next-door neighbor to quickly come inside.

"My name is Albert," he amiably asserted as he shook her soft hand gently while his eagle eyes eagerly studied the stunning Victoria intently. "A sense of serenity within your surroundings these muffins will guarantee. I honestly hope that your new house is the happiest place you will ever be.

"Only a few founders of the neighborhood in their original homes still reside. Over the many meandering years, most of them have moved away or died. You and I are the spring chickens in this significantly senior neighborhood, whose solid surroundings are safely situated where shifting sands once stood."

"My name is Victoria, and I am sincerely happy your acquaintance to make. Of your muffins or my pound cake, would you care at this time to partake? I pathetically proclaim that my front parlor remains my home's only room, that, since I moved in, has seen a much-needed mop, dustpan, and broom.

"Please sit down, Albert, and I will prepare a pot of soothing afternoon tea. I promise that it with your muffins and my pound cake truly perfect will be." They took simple pleasure in tea and treats and engaged in trivial tidbits of conversation that curiously challenged their wisdom, wills, and wits.

They revealed a resonating relaxation as Victoria served more sweets and tea, and the atmosphere in the front parlor continued to be filled with levity. The two next-door neighbors became quite noticeably and genuinely at ease and, with their congenial conversation, seemed each other to pleasantly please.

Their time together had surreally sped at such a ridiculously rapid rate that neither of them had realized it had become so ludicrously late. Albert thanked Victoria for her cordial company on this afternoon and told her he heartily hoped they would converse again very soon.

And then, as Albert stood up from Victoria's pink velvet parlor chair, he silently prayed that he would not his new neighbor severely scare when he shared something sinister that he no longer from her could hide— an appallingly alarming atrocity that years ago had taken place inside.

"A hideously horrible homicide," he confessed, "occurred within your home, in the second-floor master bedroom, where a ghost has been known to roam. A scholarly spinster was savagely strangled during that nightmarish night. The strangler then brutally beheaded her and left behind a bloody sight.

"When the police arrived and entered her darkened, death-drenched room, they vomited violently amid the viciousness that violated the virtual tomb." The crazed killer, Albert assured her, was soon apprehended, arrested, and jailed, and after being incarcerated for only one year, he died from a heart that had failed.

So extremely unseemly was the perilous picture her neighbor had just painted, Victoria fell onto her parlor floor, having forthwith formidably fainted. Albert responded to her emergency by calmly and comfortingly providing aid and carried her to the fainting couch, serenely soaked in soothing shade.

"Why did not anyone divulge the disturbing details of this terrible tale until now, after I've completely moved in?" Victoria vented as she began to wail. "It terrifies me that in the very same room where I have chosen to sleep, a wonderful woman was maliciously murdered by a maniacal, miscreant creep."

To an acutely agitated and angered Victoria, Albert ardently apologized after realizing that he had her sensibilities insensitively traumatized. He endeavored to explain that he experienced the explosively essential need, to make her aware of the dreadful details of this deeply demonic deed.

He said he was compelled to make certain that she was in the know about something surreal she might see taking on an eerily ethereal glow that could scarily share the spooky space beside her bed on random nights when the discontented, demon-dipped darkness with its sadistic stare frights.

Previous proprietresses professed that they had this phantom often seen, and the only plausible postulate for it that they could collectively glean was that the goose bump-giving, gossamer guest must surely be the ghost of the murderer who visited the crime scene only about the murder to boast.

Albert reassured Victoria that the apparition most likely meant no harm when it uttered the only word that was the cause of automatic alarm for the scared single women who at various times had lived there and with uneasy ears had heard the ghost *speak but one word, "beware!"*

After he finished telling this terrible tale, Albert left and returned home, leaving a still-shaken Victoria alone in her huge, haunted house to roam. If she would ever see the ghost, at least she had the background to know that this gaseous ghoul, most likely harmless, was neither friend nor foe.

If the ghost's purpose was to merely appear in gauzy gear and stare and softly speak the wary word of warning, which was the word *"beware,"* if she saw it, she could fearlessly fall back to the sweet safety of sleep and readily reenter a delicious dreamland after counting a hundred sheep.

Victoria thought of the extremely electric and eccentric events of the day, and afterward, felt tremendously tired and was unable any longer to stay awake, so she wearily commenced her ritual of readying herself for bed as her mind revisited repulsive reports of the wraith and the woman's head.

Despite these torturous thoughts, she slipped into sleep and drifted away and dreamily dived into delightful dalliances with pure pleasure and play. At precisely the hour of two o'clock, she woke and for the first time did see the vaporous visitor whose notorious presence was mired in murky mystery.

After sabotaging her sweet sleep, it stared at her and stood beside her bed, but she resisted the reflex to recoil because Albert had staidly said that the mysterious mist that mystically materialized likely meant no harm but merely appeared to demonstrate its desire to deliver a lifesaving alarm.

And this it did as its vibrating voice pierced and permeated the bedroom air with merely one whispered word of warning, which was the word *"beware!"* The phantasmal figure effortlessly evaporated, leaving behind not a trace of anything that would indicate it had invaded Victoria's nocturnal space.

Victoria shivered and shook after this supernaturally stupefying sighting and readily resorted to her repulsively compulsive, fidgety fingernail biting. Extremely exhausted from her eerie encounter, she shortly fell back to sleep, and for the remainder of that nightmarish night, she heard not another peep.

Over the coming weeks, the ghost did automatically and arrestingly appear, and Victoria, per her proper programming, proceeded its presence *not* to fear. The misty, mild-mannered monster mimicked a genuinely gentle gent who was conscientiously compelled one cautionary word to vigilantly vent.

Victoria and Albert had a full-fledged friendship comfortably created. It had with the passing of time genuinely and gratifyingly generated healthy helpings of happiness, companionship, dependability, and trust, which in platonic partnerships like theirs were a monumental must.

One serene summer evening after they shared a chilled cherry wine toast, an analytical Albert asked the virtuous Victoria if she had seen the ghost. She told him that it had appeared in her bedroom more than a few times and always visited at two o'clock when she heard the clock's two chimes.

The ghost displayed its daring demeanor as it hovered at her bedside. It spookily stared right at her (who, while startled, made no attempt to hide) before whispering a weighty warning through its mouth of misty air—a simple, succinct sentiment spoken with this one word, *"beware!"*

Albert was immensely relieved that Victoria had seen and already accepted the strange, otherworldly apparition, which, had it felt even a bit neglected, may have become a belligerent being with worrisome words under its breath and committed a crazed and cringe-worthy crime to cause her deliberate death.

Victoria's loveless life took a tantalizing turn when she met a handsome man whose colossally charismatic charm did instantly ignite and feverishly fan the frustratingly forgotten fire that was forced to hibernate inside her heart and prompted his marriage proposal, which promised Victoria a fresh, new start.

The couple planned to marry soon and secretly move somewhere far away and live in a magnificent mansion where their future children could play. Albert realized that his Victoria would merely remain a devoted friend, but he had always hoped their red-letter relationship would never have to end.

# Barbara Eck Tosi

Tremendously tired from the planning of her waiting-in-the-wings wedding, Victoria entered her beckoning bedroom and tenderly turned down the bedding. She fell fast asleep but suddenly awoke to sinister sounds inside her room of footsteps from a foreboding figure that now above her did lethally loom.

This non-vaporous, nocturnal newcomer had noticeably and nefariously begun to radically resemble an unhinged man who had completely come undone. He was dressed in dapper attire and sported a handsome head of dark hair. He suddenly, sharply, and succinctly spoke the one warning word, *"beware!"*

Victoria screamed shrilly as she audaciously attempted to quickly escape, but the forbidding figure's heinous hands around her narrow neck did drape. "It is I, Albert, your next-door neighbor and fond, familiar, faithful friend. I am here, my dear Victoria, to bring your full-of-promise life to an end.

"It was I who sadistically strangled and in a bout of beastliness beheaded the unsuspecting woman who, years ago, in this very same room was bedded. My distrusting twin brother, Talbert, to this house, foolishly followed me and did the murder and beheading from its beginning to end frightfully see.

"I killed and beheaded him too, so absolutely no one could ever know that I was the murderous monster responsible for this hellish horror show. The mysterious mist that you and other women have seen over the years is the ghost of my twin brother, who had tried tirelessly to tame your fears.

"He has kept careful watch over the women who have slept in this bed, ever since I strangled my first true love and chopped off her hideous head. His nebulous nighttime visits were merely meant to warn and not to scare, and that is why he chose to speak but one word, which was the word *"beware!"*

"So, my beloved Victoria, you now know the savagely sinister story of my tragic transgressions so graphically grotesque and gruesomely gory. I fell in love with you the moment we met, and I desperately wanted to be your lover, but I knew that you, in that way, were not attracted to me.

## SCARY

"I couldn't risk ruining our friendship, so I kept my feelings to myself and sealed my suffering inside a sack of scars on a special spectral shelf. You terminated our togetherness when you fancied that other man instead.

It

is

with

sadness

I

must

strangle

you

and

lop

off

your

luscious

head!"

# Family Tree

The centuries-old home held a haunting history for the unsuspecting wife and her family, who would soon be steeped in serious supernatural strife. The woman would be violently victimized that viciously cold winter day when she became the leading lady in a chillingly choreographed play.

She was on a mission to resurrect every reclusive and revered picture of her assorted ancestors, who were a mesmerizing and mercurial mixture of innate intelligence, intriguing imagination, and irrefutable insanity that formed the roots, trunk, branches, and leaves of her ancestral family tree.

She carefully climbed the deathly deep and nightmarishly narrow stairs that led to the attic cursed with a creepy and cluttered collection of wares that languished and loomed largely before her as she adeptly managed to grab onto a worn wooden beam that was dusty, dirty, and damaged.

With only one hand on the beam, she steadied her unstable stance after becoming dizzily disoriented and trapped inside a temporary trance. She released her grip on the wooden beam and approached a leather trunk, opened it, and retrieved a photo album that to the trunk's bottom had sunk.

With the album of old family photographs now safely secured in her hand, she experienced the fearful feeling that she was in complete command of ancestral memories that for centuries inside the trunk had been locked and within the parched pages of this ancient album were bafflingly blocked.

Her goal accomplished, the woman again the wooden beam did firmly grip so that her bent-over body would not teeter-totter and treacherously trip over the miscellaneous memorabilia that through the many yellowed years had witnessed her ancestors' outpourings of love, laughter, and tears.

She abruptly and absentmindedly removed her hand from the wooden beam and straightaway suffered the sick sensation of that same hand splitting a seam. Upon probing, she perceived what was plainly an insanely painful splinter barbarically buried beneath her thin skin on this demon-dipped day of winter.

# Barbara Eck Tosi

She next the nerve-numbing and netherworldly stairs daringly descended, and about her surreptitiously sinister splinter had purposely pretended to forget, as there was something secret of imminent importance pending, and it required her full participation for its successful beginning and ending.

After opening the family photo album, she experienced excruciating pain that cruelly concentrated its corruptness in the very hand and very vein where the sadistic splinter had freakishly found a perfectly pleasing place from which it could stealthily slide to her next fresh, fleshy space.

After vacating the vein in her hand, the splinter slithered up her arm, causing abnormal arterial arcing that abruptly activated an aortic alarm whose relentlessly resonating reverberations resulted in a ruinous reality when her arm morphed into the thorny branch of a terribly threatening tree.

After shocking her senseless with seismic seizures, the scary splinter sprinted to her chest, which with layers of bark was now intimately imprinted. Her tortured torso turned into a tree trunk so tormentingly tall that it obliterated the organs arranged around her aching abdominal wall.

The solitary splinter then tenaciously traveled to her rattled, remaining arm, where another branch brazenly burst forth and brought about hellacious harm to the wounded woman's brutalized body that was now electrifyingly exploding while the psychopathic splinter its surreal strength was very rapidly reloading.

Behemoth branches grew grotesquely in distinctly different directions, much like families do when seen through life's rearview reflections. From the burping bowels of brachiating branches rose reticulating leaves that camouflaged the chaos as if it were a cache concealed by thieves.

The serpent splinter seized a spot on the spirit-shaken, shuddersome stairs and resurfaced in the attic to await subsequent surges of supernatural scares. The rage-riddled remains of the wasted woman revealed a patch of pulp, which the thirsty tree trunk devilishly devoured with one gargantuan gulp.

## SCARY

The family photos flew forthwith off the yielding yellowed pages of the ancestral photo album that had seen much suffering through the ages. They buoyantly balanced themselves on the bevy of bewitching branches with the sovereign and shivering swiftness of alighting alpine avalanches.

Each photo claimed personal possession of its precious, preeminent bough, which handsomely hung amid the hierarchy of the haunting here and now. Each proudly perched upon its bough in this fascinating family tree, whose preservation would be permanently protected for all of perpetuity.

A single splinter from an old wooden beam had swiftly set into motion this enigmatic and epic birth of catastrophic confusion and caustic commotion, which coldly killed a well-meaning woman who then resurrected herself to be

the

roots,

trunk,

branches,

and

leaves

of

her

ancestral

family

tree.

# Insane Pain

Insane was the pain that plagued her psyche as she pretended not to notice.
She was savagely subjected to its sadistic storm, for which there was no poultice.
It tensely thumped and joltingly jumped from one neurotic neuron to the next,
much like a new author's nonsensical novel's clearly convoluted text.

Her pathological pain was persistently provoked, punctured, and pounded
by dangerously demonic, mercurial mutants that suspiciously surreal sounded
like hulking hunks of hissing hail hellishly hurled onto hardened concrete.
But no one knew of her persecuting pain because she kept it deceitfully discreet.

Her tears erased the fine features of her face and forced her fertile fears
to push her pulsating pain into penetrating her savagely with spears,
whose sickeningly sharp spikes were programmed to petrify their prey
with the promise of paralyzation to persons preventing their diabolic display.

She was cruelly cloistered inside a churning cistern of convulsing pain,
whose flagrantly frightening, fanatically fractious, and fulminating refrain
forced her pathetically perishable psyche to fidget, flounder, and flail,
and succumb to sleepless situations that radically rendered her pitifully pale.

Her hideously, horribly, hurting head became the harrowingly herculean size
of a hot air balloon besieged by boisterous breezes and brazen skies.
Her miserably muddled and meandering mind torturously trembled and throbbed
and blindly and brainlessly bounced like a tennis ball lopsidedly lobbed.

An eccentric example of stoicism this woman had allowed herself to become.
Her pursuit of pain was precisely patterned after stoics who had grown numb
from making sure the masochistic machinations of their pain did not show
because stoics at no time permit the world their penchant for pain to know.

Strangely stranded inside a self-imposed sinkhole of insatiable pain, she searched for a center stage that she, through her pain, could gain. She would never risk losing the only reason for living her anguished life—

her

pain

to

which

she

was

morbidly

married

and

loved

as

a

man

loves

his

wife.

# Gnome Gnightmare

The cleverly camouflaged cottage was the cold color of cucumber green, a shade selected to shield its shuddersome savageness from being seen by the prying pupils of passersby who crept inside this cryptic corridor of frightful forest fiendishly fraught with a fathomlessly foliaged floor.

Inside the well-disguised woodland cottage, there dwelled a giant gnome. For many a year, he had made this restful retreat his hideaway home. This gruesome gnome was known to own an appetite supernaturally scary. He lived alone because he deboned all gnomes who nearby did tarry.

Within the wild and woolly woodland, this wicked wretch terrified the worry-warted gnomes who sickeningly sensed his surreptitious stride. They fled to their knee-high gnome homes like a horde of hungry horseflies eagerly en route to a pastoral picnic promising a pleasing plethora of pies.

The gnomes' nerves were in knots, and each hid his or her frightened face until certain this crazed creature had, at last, ceased his chilling chase of each unlucky gnome he had chosen to catch and kill for his lunch with one casual, carnivorous, cannibalistic, and cataclysmic crunch.

It would require but one bolt of lively lightning, boldly brilliant, to prove that this ghastly gnome to deadly danger was not resilient by orchestrating his immediate death due to nature's natural electrocution, for which he would be unable to implement any form of retaliatory retribution.

The sky's bleak and blossoming blackness boldly beckoned the belligerent rain to fall fiercely and focus fully on torturing the terrified, timorous terrain. With alarmingly accelerating anxiety, the nerve-numbed gnome readily realized that he—with full-fledged, free-falling fear—was permanently paralyzed.

Lightning lurked above the lawless landscape, where thunder would soon follow before he arrived at his cucumber-green cottage inside the heather-laced hollow. Hyperventilating with horror, he headed homeward in a horrendously huge hurry as his cowardly countenance exhibited electrifyingly excessive worry.

# Barbara Eck Tosi

He fitfully fretted over the fatal fact that he had miserably missed his cue when he did the nervous gnomes calculatingly chase, corner, catch, and chew. The time he took to track and tackle each temptingly tantalizing treat could very well his search for survival in this formidable forest defeat.

On wickedly wet and deathly dangerous leaves, he slid and seriously slipped and subsequently stumbled on a strangely shaped stump over which he tripped. As the rainstorm relished its raucous rants, the gnome did fumble and flail on this rabid, ruthless, rain-ravaged, and worrisomely wild woodland trail.

His cucumber-green cottage stood squarely in his soggy and squinty sights. If he could courageously conquer his cursed case of the very scary frights, he might outrun the lightning and thunder and arrive safely at his home. If he failed to accomplish this feat, he was doomed to be a *dead* gnome.

He recklessly ran through the unrepentant rain that resolutely retained its roar and eventually found his hysterical self standing in front of his cottage door. He was exhausted but beyond ready to unlock the lifesaving latch that steadfastly secured the stalwart door that stood beneath the roof of thatch.

But as he reached inside the puddles that posed as his pants pockets, his waterlogged eyes disgustingly dislodged from their super slippery sockets. The cottage's key, which he professed was inside his pocket, was positively not, so he surmised with shock that he was solidly stuck in a seriously unsafe spot.

He realized that his key had fallen out of his pocket and gone freely flying while he was acutely absorbed in his devotion to desperately trying to rapidly run from the wet, withered leaves and strangely shaped stump that had culminated in his being catapulted onto his wide, wart-ridden rump.

Lightning appeared and laughingly leered at the gnome deeply dipped in dread, and with its sadistic savagery, it straightaway struck him undeniably dead. His brutalized body from the lethal lightning was beyond being badly burned, but one brave gnome ventured out and, with much joy, a surprise discerned.

Due to a trick of twisted fate that was deeply desirable and most incredible, the gnome's remains were—remarkably, albeit eerily—entirely edible. Hungry gnomes enjoyed every irresistible inch of this wretched beast that plentifully provided them and their families with a fully fortifying feast.

The cucumber-green cottage that had been the solitary sanctuary and home of this dark, dangerous, disgusting, diabolic, and grotesquely giant gnome, was, into a beauteous bed-and-breakfast for nomadic gnomes magically made

and

spiritedly

celebrated

with

a

warm,

welcoming,

woodland-wide,

gnome

parade.

# Criminally Corporate

I was flush with the floor by the foul finish of the deeply disturbing day because I had, a multitude of malignant times, managed to scarily stray into the pompous and perilous paths of career-climbing, corporate whores who splintered my spine with each shameless slam of their supercilious doors.

Throughout the day, they forced me to display an insulting sign that read: *Walk ruthlessly all over me until I'm definitively declared dead.* Their spiteful spit and merciless mockery knocked me to the wooden floor, where they used and abused my body until there was little left to restore.

They readily, rudely, repugnantly, and repeatedly refused to recognize me, and this aching absence of acknowledgment arrested my ability to flee. When I ardently attempted my acutely adulterated anatomy to animate, I was coldcocked again by corporate cutthroats coexisting with caustic hate.

My accumulating agony accelerated as each savagely spiked and hellish heel punctured and penetrated my pathetic person to the point I could not feel the predacious pain they insanely inflicted because I'd become so numb and by debilitating delirium was deviously and deliberately overcome.

Despite the savages' storm-squalled schedules being suffocatingly tight, they still had time to egotistically engage in a frenzied, fatalistic fight to finish first in their compulsively competitive and criminally corporate race and fixate on fiendish formulas to black out my body and erase my face.

They seriously sensed that their star-studded status and self-satisfying worth were automatically assigned to them at the monumental moment of their birth and that their sacred social standing needed to be regularly reemphasized to solidly safeguard the selfish superiority that they sanctimoniously prized.

Seismically smarter and titanically taller these anal animals aimed to appear as they sadistically sought my suffering soul to solidly saturate with fear. Formidably flatter and significantly sadder my browbeaten body became as it took on the look of a pallid portrait, purposeless without its frame.

# Barbara Eck Tosi

My fragmented flesh became fluid and flowed, and my solubilized scars wept
onto the floor and below where through the subterranean sprawl they crept
into the unseemly underground inundated with dirty drains and smelly holes
and mingled with mammoth mice, robust rats, and morbidly macabre moles.

Their tongues penetrated the pool that previously posed as my body parts.
After much licking, their rears rejoiced by ripping lethally long-lasting farts.
The pitifully paltry pool that remained was patently paraded away
by sweet and sour sewage advertising the many meals eliminated that day.

My physical body had been mercilessly massacred and eternally extinguished,
but my sweet, soulful spirit would never be desecrated, disrupted, or diminished.
On the wicked, wooden floor where my blacklisted body at one time did lay,
a sparkling sphere abruptly appeared and did brilliantly back and forth sway.

To a mellow medieval melody, it daintily danced with a mystical moth
and radiantly rose above a glimmering, shimmering, sweetly seductive swath
of pearlized purple pansies that punctuated the poetically powerful place
with a blindingly beautiful brilliance that no one and nothing could ever erase.

In the blizzard-like blast of dizzy days and weary years that thereafter followed,
the speed walkers in sick, stiff, snobbish superiority superficially wallowed.
As they religiously retraced their sinfully self-absorbed steps each defiant day,
they doggedly dug their dark, devilish heels into their prospective prey.

They wretchedly wedged their witchy way into extraordinarily early graves
reserved for them inside the cold confines of contaminated cobwebbed caves
where the munching maggots, narcissistic nematodes, and restless roaches waited
for the devil's invitation-only introduction, ironically and irrevocably ill-fated.

Anorexic from the accumulated ages of appalling agony and abhorrent abuse,
the wooden floor, corrupted to its cancerous core, caved in and cut loose,
and the criminally corporate, career-climbing whores wearing their preppy shoes

descended

to

their

deaths

in

diabolic

darkness

to

decompose

inside

doomsday

ooze.

# Clever Concealment

The man was a fetching fellow, dapperly dressed and gloriously groomed. These descriptions demonstrate why the dwellers in this tiny town assumed that he had amassed abundant assets, including significant sums of money, and subsisted in a splendid sphere, sublimely sweetened with sugar and honey.

He walked with measured, methodical steps, seemingly without thinking. His focused eyes were ferally fixed and noticeably never blinking. His mechanical movements mimicked motions rehearsed and precisely planned, to the point that they appeared abnormally awkward and uncannily canned.

His steady stream of superlative silk shirts and strikingly similar silk ties revealed a richness that reinforced people's penchant to summarily surmise that he was a genteel gentleman who lived the quintessential *good life*—alone, they presumed, as they never noticed him in the company of a wife.

Mystifying monotony mirrored itself in his motionless and matter-of-fact face. Public prattle permeated the places where he pursued his perfect pace. The disclosure, however, of one destination was doomed to remain a mystery—an unsettling *unknown* about this man's unusually unapparent history.

His mammoth mansion hugged the harrowing hillside and freakishly flaunted a chilling creepiness that immediately indicated it might be horribly haunted. No one could collect the considerable courage to venture anywhere near this particularly peculiar place that aroused uneasiness and forbidding fear.

The mysterious man was excessively enamored with his eccentric, exotic plants, which regularly received regal care revealed in their superior stance. Inside a splayed, sun-saturated coffin, they fervently and fabulously flourished because they were with prized premium fertilizer noticeably nourished.

The favorable fertilizer fueled the foliage's fondness for feminine creatures, one of which rotted beneath rapacious roots that ravaged her fading features. The man's first wife it was whose remains had been deliciously decaying, ever since the day he had deliberately delighted in her sadistic slaying.

Over her remnants of rotting rankness, filthy flies were pathologically playing and eating, excreting, and an eerie entourage of eldritch eggs ludicrously laying. The eggs excitedly into slimy, slippery, squirming maggots maliciously turned and blissfully burrowed into the man's brain where his blatant bloodlust burned.

His first wife woefully turned out to be not at all like what he had expected, which was why he'd decided her disappointing self must be radically rejected. He strangled her with one of his seriously sick, sinful, savage silk ties and then used portions of her putrefying parts as the mincemeat for his pies.

He didn't bake the pies as he enjoyed eating them room-temperature raw, which was the way he consumed his food, especially food he cut with a saw— his cringe-worthy, calamitous chainsaw that (with its blistering, bellicose buzz) absolutely assured the destruction of everything and everyone that was.

No one ever came close to discovering the one secret and secure location to which the man wittingly walked with deliberate, daily dedication. It was a peculiarly private place with secrets so frighteningly forbidden that it remained from public view inexplicably inaccessible and hidden.

In this perversely protected place, the man's other wives lay without life, morbidly murdered in the same way as his first witless and worthless wife. These previous, purposeless partners were placed below pretty potted plants

inside

cobwebbed

coffins

besieged

by

restless

## SCARY

roaches,

maggots,

and

ants.

# Slumber Party

To the Saturday-night slumber party hosted by my favorite friend, I was politely invited and, with abundant anticipation, did attend. Eleven girls joined us, and we became a thick-as-thieves thirteen ladies lured by the looming *later* of this eerie evening yet unseen.

We slouched inside our sleeping bags and spoke in a senseless fashion and devoured jet-fueled junk food, which was our private passion. Our demureness dramatically disappeared in this festive atmosphere of strong and solid sisterhood that staunchly shielded us from fear.

We gussied up in glamorous gowns that were fabulously fancy and frilly and wildly wiggled and girlishly giggled until we became seriously silly. Our bulging bellies were bouncing, and our rampant rowdiness was real. We were tenacious teenagers who every gigabyte of our girlhood did feel.

We playfully plopped ourselves down and properly propped our heads up and watched super scary movies as we ate popcorn from a plastic cup. We stayed awake by slurping sodas from many a supermarket can that contained considerable caffeine and sugar, which a teen's fire fan.

When the last horror movie had ended, my faithful friend did implore us to move quickly and quietly to the entrance of a disturbing door that opened, she alleged, onto strangely steep and squeaky stairs that led the way to a deserted attic full of old, wooden rocking chairs.

The door had long ago been locked, and the attic creepily quiet had been since the original homeowners died amid a severely startling, swirling spin of rampant rumors, gossip-garbled guesses, and fantastical fairy-tale lore that kept this dormant door locked and bolted for at least a century or more.

After explaining the elusive events that led to the disturbing door's locking, our slumber party planner proposed something shudderingly shocking. Pay close attention now to her words upon which she coughed and choked and the radical response that these same words in me piercingly provoked.

"The abandoned attic full of old rocking chairs that beyond the staircase glares
has not a chance of ever being seen unless one of you dauntlessly dares
to unlock the door, ascend the steep stairs, and rock on the old rocking chairs,
all the while remaining ridiculously oblivious to all of earth's external cares.

"Upon completion of the rocking and without any of the old chairs mocking,
the self-controlled soul must then remove and leave one woolen stocking
for the frostbitten rats, goose-bumped bats, and ice cream-cold cats
that struggle to survive in this arctic attic without mittens, scarves, and hats.

"After terminating this tedious task, she, wearing one warm woolen stocking,
must discreetly descend the sinister stairs without undertaking any talking,
walk through the other side of the door she earlier unlocked and entered,
and before us authentically appear—unannounced, unaffected, and centered."

After being chillingly challenged with this task teeming with total terror,
I felt compelled to be this slumber party's sole challenge bearer.
"I'll accept," I immediately said, "this mother of all dangerous dares."
So, I unlocked and unbolted the disturbing door and ascended the scary stairs.

I did, without the chairs mocking, on every old rocker begin my rocking,
and upon finishing this tiresome task, I left behind one woolen stocking.
But then, as I began to descend the steep stairs without any talking,
I suddenly became a horrified victim of suspiciously surreptitious stalking.

The cold killer rats, bats, and cats, with their monstrously maniacal motions
over my surprised, single-stockinged body, perversely poured poisonous potions.
Their evil eyes, Satan souls, and hellishly hardened hideous hearts
positively proved their patent participation in the darkest of demonic arts.

The rats, bats, and cats upon my petrified person did pronouncedly pounce—
an accelerated action that I accurately ascertained did absolutely announce
their intention to rip apart my flesh into particularly pleasing parts
to be penetrated by pursuing projectiles—designated as death-dealing darts.

# SCARY

The devastatingly destructive darts into my fragments of flesh were flung. They looked like torturous, tungsten-tipped toothpicks that tenaciously clung to the remnants of me that were served up as high-class hors d'oeuvres smeared with a savory sauce showcasing my tissues, bones, and nerves.

My life was destined for decimation when I deliberately danced with a dare and subsequently into the vile eyes of dark demons did so sickeningly stare. Their irreverent, insanely insatiable, and inauspiciously induced interference precipitated my pitifully predetermined and painfully permanent disappearance.

The rats, bats, and cats shape-shifted my stockings into warm woolen wraps. They luridly licked their Luciferian lips and took ludicrously long naps, during which they deliriously dreamed about the devilishly delicious buffet

that

would

be

catered

by

their

next

unsettlingly

upended

prey.

# High Tea

The long-lived, loquacious ladies luxuriated in chairs whose backs were high and unsparingly upholstered in voluptuous velvet, which did immediately imply that this tearoom with wallpapered walls and windows of stunning stained glass welcomed wealthy women who were composites of considerable cash and class.

Crystal chandeliers cast candescent light onto the copiously conspicuous ceiling that resonated with resolute regality while resplendently and reverently revealing its particularly prominent position above the aloofly aristocratic atmosphere that throughout the intoxicating tearoom did with abundant ambiance appear.

The silver-spooned socialites sported scalps swathed in soft, silky hair in scintillating shades of predetermined purple that prompted people to stare. Preeminent parlors placed purple pigments in their prestigious potpourri of preparations professed to be a privileged person's perfect cup of tea.

The octogenarians wore outfits ornamented with sequins and luscious laces. Bright berry blush beautified the cheeks of their fragile, fine-china faces. Luxurious lilac lipstick layered their lips with a scintillating sheen that, outside of movie stars' celebrated circles, was seldom, if ever seen.

Their premier perfumes possessed posh notes of patchouli that did pose with lavender, lotus, lily of the valley, lobelia, and the rest of those other soul-soothing and snobby scents that quite dramatically drew the absolute attention of the noble noses into which the sweet smells blew.

Their highbrow heads held hoity-toity hats festooned with frills that included fine, fancy feathers, glittering gemstones, and riveting ribbons regularly alluded to in the eye-popping, jaw-dropping, drama-dripping, and deeply delicious pages of glamour magazines ravenously read and remembered by women of all ages.

Grandiose gloves graced their hoary hands and hid offensive, old-age spots that curiously copycatted the corrupted color of climate-corroded clay pots. The patrons prized their panache-punctuated pearls and divinely designed dresses and previously pointed out handsome hats that enhanced their purple tresses.

## Barbara Eck Tosi

On classically crustless, tantalizing triangles of tempting tearoom breads
clothed in cream cheese, chicken salad, and other splendiferous spreads,
the lovely ladies leisurely lunched while consumed by courtly conversation,
complimenting each other's ostentatious outfits with ample admiration.

They supped on sinfully swanky soups and sipped steaming cups of tasty tea,
and ceremoniously savored sweet, sumptuous scones with long-lasting levity.
They proudly publicized being proper persons of privilege, prestige, and power,
who solely subsisted inside the superior interiors of many an ivory tower.

The tearoom remarkably reflected a sensational splash of stupendous splendor
that the spirited season of cherished Christmas does so remarkably render.
It was ever so emphatically evidenced in the spectacularly special places
where love, peace, hope, and joy unassumingly unveiled their faithful faces.

The parting pots of holiday tea were perfectly prepared and properly placed
on all the lovely luncheon tables after being lusciously and lavishly laced
with a highly lively liquid so obviously outrageous and deliciously divine
it rivaled every bottle of regal, refined, and ridiculously rare wine.

In his secret subterranean cellar, the tearoom proprietor privately kept
a substantial stash of spirited sauce, which he surreptitiously spawned and schlepped.
The audaciously ample samples of his folksy, festive, fermented cheer
adequately assuaged his alcohol addiction for one memorably merry year.

Bountiful batches of this blissful beverage he benevolently set aside
so that he during the Christmas high tea could it inside the teapots hide
and then wonderfully witness the grown-up girls gregariously giggle and laugh
as if they had been splendidly soaking in a sparkling champagne bath.

After climbing out of their high-back chairs, the well-to-do women tried
to stave off stubborn stumbles and slips while managing to gingerly guide
one another out of the teeter-tottering tearoom's dizzyingly distorted door
as they steeped in hallucinogenic happiness never known to them before.

The proprietor closed the tipsy tearoom for the remainder of the merry day and polished off the pots of potent tea that on the luncheon tables still lay. His staggering surprise sanctioned these sassy seniors to have a blessed ball.

This

event

was,

truth

be

told,

the

Christmas

"high"

tea

after

all!

# Thoughtless

I had a thought that thoughtlessly tarried and totally transformed my brain
into a considerably confusing conglomeration of clutter categorically insane.
It completely controlled my cerebral cortex, which forestalled my forgetting
the turbulence within my thought brought on by brutal, brain bloodletting.

A second thought turbulently thrashed about and wiggled its wretched way
next to my first thought, which energetically engaged in egotistical play
with my second thought, attempting with its lunatic lexicon to overtly outsize
my first thought—both literarily lily-gilding their way to a Pulitzer Prize.

A troubling third thought tried to toss my first and second thoughts away,
but the first two thoughts tricked the third thought into allowing them to stay.
*Each thought thought the other thoughts* ridiculously and recklessly rambled
and spawned ceaseless cerebral storms symbolic of eggs savagely scrambled.

My mercilessly muddled merry-go-round mind was unable to hide and hush
my three tenaciously traveling thoughts that next to one another did brush.
Ten other thoughts triggered a tsunami that into my think tank rushed in,
sending my original three thoughts into a seriously spiraling and sadistic spin.

My toxically thickening thoughts touched off a tornado that furiously funneled
into the crevices of my corpus callosum, where all my thoughts then tunneled
through my twisted and tangled thalamus, torturously trying to finally find
a workable way for this wicked whirlwind to unequivocally unwind.

I felt defenselessly deflated and defeated like a rebel rose without a thorn.
I wistfully wished my tumultuous, truncated thoughts had never been born.
Marred by maleficence, my meninges were unprecedentedly unprotective;
thus, making materializing mental mergers nerve-numbingly nonelective.

I could not thwart my thoughts from spontaneously screaming and scheming.
Not one of my trespassing thoughts was with tolerance or tenderness teeming.
I needed to manage or murder the meaningless mixing and mindless matching
that they madly maneuvered while other thoughts were exponentially hatching.

The terrorizing tornadoes, titanic tsunamis, scrambled eggs, and broken shells that fiercely forced my traumatizing thoughts to hide inside their separate hells, succumbed to their psychotic spinelessness on that shuddersome, scary day,

when

I

tormentingly

terminated

all

of

them

by

totally

thinking

them

away.

# Mr. Bartoni's Bakery

Bartoni's Bakery was a saccharine staple in this small, sweet-toothed town, where sinfully sublime, superbly sugared specimens stymied every frown. A sunshiny smile surfaced each time someone savored the seductive sweets, which connoisseurs of confection called the crème de la crème of Italian treats.

The bakery boasted its renowned reputation known throughout the world as the sole sweet shop where satisfied customers' toes compulsively curled whenever their taste buds were tickled by the delectables they ingested, ensuring that their stomachs with solid sweetness were sensationally infested.

One day while Mr. Bartoni was baking blueberry biscotti and pecan pies, the hell-bent health inspector arrived with his covert clan of culinary spies. They comprehensively checked the conditions of the confectionary's operation and detailed all desirable and disconcerting discoveries in their documentation.

The bakery was commendably close to passing its annual health inspection until the team discovered a deeply disturbing and disgusting reflection of rampant, repulsive, ripe, and relentlessly reeking rodent droppings in a mirror mounted above an amazing assortment of cake toppings.

The irate inspector berated the baker while barking his belligerent orders that mandated Mr. Bartoni straightaway set traps to kill the rodent boarders. Their menacing mixture of moist and dry droppings could catastrophically cause deadly diseases that were dying to put people's lives on a permanent pause.

Bartoni's Bakery was publicly proclaimed pathogenic and permanently closed. This predicament a profoundly painful problem for the blacklisted baker posed. He endlessly endured excruciating episodes of officiously omnipresent oppression and soon spiraled into a suffocating state of devastatingly debilitating depression.

Meanwhile, the hardened health inspector was accorded an admirable award, planned to be presented to him soon by the town's stalwart sanitation board. A celebration complete with classic cuisine was created for this crowning event, which would commence inside a country estate open to every gal and gent.

The stomachs of socialites and commoners both were giddily guaranteed to hurt after they enjoyed an all-you-can-eat buffet and a one-of-a-kind dessert. A gala this grand had not garnered such glory since the mayor had married an award-winning author whose noteworthy name considerable clout carried.

As the board revisited the reality that Bartoni's Bakery was forever closed, a daunting dilemma for their muscle-flexing members was painfully posed. The nearest bakery open for business was five hundred miles from this town. This nagging, negative news netted each board member a flustered frown.

During an emergency board meeting, the members centered their discussions on their options for holding this affair without any regretful repercussions. After a day of dogged deliberations, they reached a disconcerting decision, set into motion after being stamped with their signature, sanitized precision.

As the clock ticked and tocked, the board president called Mr. Bartoni and begged the banned baker to, *for this one and one time only,* temporarily reopen his boarded-up bakery for the sole purpose of creating a cake for the health inspector whose award they would be celebrating.

He reminded Mr. Bartoni that all rats and rat droppings must be gone, as there was no time for another inspection with everything else going on. He then instructed him to make a cake unlike any he had before baked—one whose taste bud-teasing, gut-pleasing properties could never be faked.

To Mr. Bartoni, the sanitation board president made it categorically clear that upon completion of *this* special cake, *no other confections could appear* in the front window or on the shelves of this once-idolized Italian baker whose purpose in life had perished inside a sweet, simple, sugar shaker.

The day before the august arrival of this anxiously anticipated event, Mr. Bartoni to his achingly abandoned and boarded-up bakery went. He ignored the president's order to get rid of rat droppings and rats as he had the inspector's original command issued over icing in vats.

After he pried open the bakery's door, he saw the rats that had destroyed his reputation, career, and life and had the townspeople aptly annoyed. The sweets that had satisfied the bakery patrons' confectionary cravings had been ripped away, resulting in their resentment-riddled ravings.

Mr. Bartoni eyeballed the evidentiary excrement existing in the same place, where it, the health inspector, and his team had first come face-to-face. New dewy droppings were also displayed inside the banned building's interior. These fresh feces would foster the creation of a cake splendidly superior.

The baker had particularly perfect plans for these rat droppings, fresh and old. He would add them to this cake and frosting for epicurean experiences bold. The decadent dried droppings he stealthily into a shatter-proof shaker placed—one that with sugar and fabulous flavors had already been lavishly laced.

The fact that the fresh fecal droppings so forthrightly fruitful were convinced Mr. Bartoni the complete collection into his cake batter to stir. The subsequent slime was surreally sublime and, when baked, would enhance this gala's glitz and glamour, guaranteed the guests to eternally entrance.

The designated day duly arrived, as did the guests in their attire most flattering. Proudly present and puffed up were the health inspector and his smattering of stiff, stuffy, salty, secretive, and sadistically sanitary sidekicks, all of whom soon would radically regret giving the cake's icing so many licks.

The health inspector thanked the townspeople, all of whom this party attended. Mr. Bartoni bit his bitter baker's tongue and then torturously ascended to a level that enabled him to elevate the ego of the inspector with words that effortlessly exited his mannerly mouth like the breath of beautiful birds.

This one-of-a-kind, killer cake with its rich, regal rat droppings reigned. The draw of this drop-dead delicious dessert could never be forced or feigned. The cake was so mouthwateringly moist its tender texture bordered on batter, and its phenomenally fabulous frosting created cause for concentrated chatter.

# Barbara Eck Tosi

A more artistic, avant-garde cake there had in this arresting arena never been. Cutting it could certainly be construed as committing a majorly mortal sin. But cut it they did into symmetrical slices following the conclusion of dinner, before the inspector was slated to speak about being such a worthy winner.

After the last piece of the baker's cake had been systematically sliced and served, everyone and everything inside the estate suddenly swiveled and swerved. The dizzy diners vomited vitriolic volumes of the celebratory cake. Disturbingly disoriented, they slipped on their spew and did severely shake.

They straightaway suffered seismic seizures and were smothered in sickly spots that resembled repulsively red and prominently purple polka dots. Every man, woman, and child was cursed with fiery fevers and severe shock and unable to escape the hovering hands of death's diabolical doomsday clock.

The motley lot of merrymakers immediately lapsed into irreversible comas, after which they barely twitched and soon died amid the atrocious aromas that hemorrhagic fever with hideous horridness does hellaciously bring to those whose sticky stomachs to robust rat droppings do conscientiously cling.

The health inspector, who had selfishly scarfed down more than one cake slice, was particularly punished by personally paying the pathetic and painful price for the ego-erasing, confidence-negating, and deep, devastating disgrace that he with his deeply demoralizing drama had caused Mr. Bartoni to face.

His sugary sanctuary once saturated with a satisfyingly sweet perfection, did, with one insignificant, insulting, irreverent, and ill-intended inspection, instantly become the sordid and sensationalized site of rat dropping detection that branded his bakery the birthplace of an insidious and irreversible infection.

After all the partiers had officially perished, the country estate was burned. Such was the plan of this brilliant baker who had been savagely spurned. Once the ashes had settled, he called the mayor of a neighboring town and told him that a fatal fever and fire had brought his beloved town down.

The baker's call focused on the fact that *he*, fortunately, had not fallen victim to the disease that left the rest dead like bees deprived of pollen. Their bodies were burned in a ferocious fire that had forever sealed their fate by reducing them to amalgamated ashes inside the bowels of the country estate.

Mr. Bartoni begged the mortified, mystified mayor to super speedily spread the word that all residents of the baker's town had been duly declared dead. He informed him that the former owners' homes remained in mint conditions and were immediately available to house the mayor's assortment of additions.

Upon their arrival, the noteworthy newcomers could stake their rightful claims to the property and possessions of previous owners who had perished in flames. The handsome homes would provide generations with renewed prestige and power that hemorrhagic fever and fire had destroyed during the town's final hour.

Established enterprises eagerly offered their brick-and-mortar embraces to the daring, departing denizens with discernible determination on their faces. These excited entrepreneurs were effortlessly energized and instantly inspired to move away from the mundane jobs of which they had grown torturously tired.

Parties of plain and pedigreed people with promises of prized prosperity came, their free homes, free businesses, and free-spiritedness to quickly claim. The ironic icing on the iconic cake was that Mr. Bartoni's bakery had survived. Never again would he of his confections, credentials, and creativity be deprived.

Mr. Bartoni befittingly became the most beloved baker in the known world. People again savored his sumptuous sweets as their toes compulsively curled. He readily regained the renowned reputation he had long ago rightfully earned

before

the

health

inspector
and
his
tyrannical
team
of
the
rat
droppings
had
first
learned.

# Imagine That

The school day ended as the blaring bell announced it was three o'clock. Out of their crowded and chaotic classrooms, students began to wildly walk. Hastening down the hectic hallways, they focused on the forthcoming fun they would seize since the schizophrenic school day was officially done.

But one gloomy girl's misdirected mind was relentlessly and ruinously racing as she in the hooks of a harrowing hallway was blindly back and forth pacing. Held hostage by exponentially escalating academic expectations, she endured habitual, horrendous, and hideously heavy heart palpitations.

The following day she would be forced four frightening exams to face if she could not convince just one of her teachers to temporarily erase the painful persecution pursuing her by postponing one exam for one day—an act that would her aimlessly adrift anxiety astronomically allay.

The girl's predisposition toward paranoia put her on a perilous path leading to terrifying tests in English, German, history, and math. Four exams on one day could cause chaos of the cataclysmic kind—one that radically reiterated the reason she rapid relief must find.

Not one of her four teachers would oblige her with the opportune okay to take one of the excruciatingly exigent exams on a different day. They had already raced to restful retreats to reap *their* ritualistic release, leaving her stranded inside a scary scene quite unlikely to ever cease.

She was silently suffocating inside a sick space that spontaneously fell into the deep, dark dominion of a dry, deserted, and deadly well. Anxiety agitated her atrophying anatomy's each neurotic nerve ending that debilitating depression was desperately and deliberately befriending.

As the girl dizzily and dishearteningly down the daunting hallway walked, she spookily sensed that she by something supernatural was being stalked. She stopped suddenly and turned around, but upon seeing no one there, she continued her worrisome walk with an overly abundant amount of care.

# Barbara Eck Tosi

Her forbidding feelings of being followed finally forced her to peek inside the empty classrooms to find the someone she now heard speak. As she searched the remaining classroom, she was startled by the voice of a woman sitting in a chair as if in possession of this only choice.

"Not one person ever noticed that you were bloodcurdlingly boiling inside an academically ambitious teapot where you were tirelessly toiling to keep your head above the pernicious pressure and maniacal madness," the woman told the grave girl in a tone soaked in a sickening sadness.

"For many miserable years, you have reaped the wrath of a ruinous ruse that lethally led you to a scholarly life that you did neither want nor choose. I have come to transport you to a serene space," she steadfastly said, "where you will be able to eternally escape your debilitating and deadly dread.

"In this secure and secret place, your imagination will regally reign. It will possess the power to personally persecute with palpable pain the idiotic, irrational individuals who have for so long deserved to feel the grisly glue you will gleefully use their fate for all time to seal.

"You may conjure up any calamity that will most completely ensure the piercing, penetrating, and pulsating pain that the perpetrators will endure. You may saturate your selected scenarios with satisfyingly sadistic scenes and expeditiously eradicate insignificant existences by using any means."

Without warning, the woman vanished inside a mystically manipulated mist that spontaneously segued into a secret space after a curiously quirky twist. Gone for good, the woman was, and her voice would never again be heard, but the girl listened intently to her message and memorized it word for word.

Her invincible intrepidness instantly ignited her irrepressible imagination, which tenaciously tackled a ten-ton teapot's colossally complex construction, top-loaded it with weighty water and straightaway strategically steadied it on a behemoth Bunsen burner that, with hideously high heat, had been readied.

# SCARY

She tetchily treated her terrible teachers to a bumpy and bruising bus ride. After they achingly arrived at the school, she ordered them to strictly abide by *her* rules as she was immersed in immediately and irreversibly investing *her* efforts to expose each of them to *her* terrifying techniques of testing.

The girl forced her teachers to enter the school and follow her to the room, where, earlier, her illustrious imagination had erupted into full bloom. She irritably instructed each one to sit in an uncomfortable student seat and read the books that rested on the racks above their trepidatious feet.

The ten-ton teapot had been transported to the treacherous top of a deadly desk, behind which these teachers once sat cultivating curricula quite Kafkaesque. The water inside the titanic tea kettle curtly came to a belligerent boil as the teachers, badgered by boring books, curled up into a claustrophobic coil.

In this room, they would remain until the girl decided she would dismiss them—twelve torturous years after they first heard the taunting teapot hiss. During that threatening time, thousands of tests they would be forced to take, achingly absent all ability their asphyxiating anxiety to subdue or shake.

The girl imagined that twelve years had passed, and it was now time to place her teachers into the boiling water, their lives to permanently erase. Their bodies bulleted to the bottom where their flesh, blistered and burned, pulled away from their hard-boiled bones and into traces of teachers turned.

The remnants of these reprobate rejects readily rendered a bitterly brewed beverage boasting it could be daintily drunk or cannibalistically chewed. The girl's ingenious, irresistibly irreverent, and indestructible imagination had creatively concocted this curriculum-cursed, teacher-tortured tea creation.

Her tenebrous thoughts had twistedly triggered many a taboo emotion and quickly quieted the quintessential confusion and the corrosive commotion that, like scary, skulking shadows, stalked her sanity with such surreal fear that it sadistically suffocated her shuttered psyche year after year after year.

This serene sanctuary sweetly spawned a stationary and soul-saving cease to her tangible terror now triumphantly transcended by penetrating peace. Her imagination illustriously instigated rebellion-rooted, radioactive revenge on the terminally tarnished teachers whom she was compelled to abysmally avenge.

Aneurysms advanced upon academia's arteries in an aggressively acerbic way. Exams became extinct when their entrails eroded beneath the deadly decay of insanely insensitive teachers whose sick strategies had long symbolized everything evoking the endless evilness the tormented girl deeply despised.

The recycled rage that reverberated through the ruined regions of her brain and chillingly choked every cherished chance of her becoming certifiably sane could now be unnoticeably unleashed in a creatively convincing way

by

her

intoxicating

imagination

inspired

to

have

the

irresistible

last

say.

# Death Rhyme

Beneath the buckled, brittle-boned bridge acutely and audibly anguished,
the liquid lines of longevity listlessly lingered, labored, and languished
in their powerlessness to penetrate a place where permanent peace fused
with silken serenity and soulful solace in stationary spaces seldom used.

Honeysuckle huddled inside the hushed hills of its humble hideaway,
actively avoiding the dark, deadly demons on this day of defiant decay
in which time timidly traveled within a dismally defined, deadened space
and a sickened sunflower shriveled and fatally fell onto its faded face.

Parched primrose perilously peeked at a sizzling swath of sun-scorched sky
while lilac lobelia lethally leaned against a corpse flower destined to die
beside painfully pale and panting peonies, petunias, pansies, and phlox
that suffered the same stream's steam that stalked the hiding hollyhocks.

The disheartened dahlias dizzily drooped in a deliberate and dreary daze
as they dangerously drifted below the heinous, heat-hypnotized haze.
Cursed camellias crouched in a corner amid the thirsty thistle and thyme,
while trillium and delphinium died inside a deeply disturbing death rhyme.

Hopeless heather held hostage by the harsh, hostile, hell-soaked weather
delved into a daunting diatribe with a sweat-streaked, sun-stroked feather.
Anxious asters were agonizingly asphyxiated by August's evil entourage
of historic heat waves that did the loitering landscape lethally barrage.

Inside an incandescent ingress, irises were inundated with intolerable rays
that wilted their waning whispers and wiped out their remaining days.
Gentle jasmine, joltingly jeopardized by the sinister sun's sudden spin,
burned on the blistered battlefield in a wicked war it could never win.

Helpless heliotrope suffered strangulation by a tensely twisted rope
of unyielding English ivy exhaustingly enveloped in extinguishing hope.
Aching amaranth was agonizingly ablated by the sear of a slithering snake
that slimily serpentined its way into the boiling bowels of a languid lake.

Little lamb's ears and newborn baby's tears harassed by the hideous heat bawled with the blissless buttercups brought down in blatant, broiling defeat. Temperature-tortured tuberoses were threateningly thrust into a toppling tizzy, while delicate daisies disastrously dwindled as if they were drunk and dizzy.

Severely scalded was the wailing water writhing inside the screaming stream that held its bemoaning breath when hunted by the hissing, homicidal steam. The desolation was dictated by a disordered desperation that cruelly caused death to destroy the sacred space where liquid longevity had briefly paused.

Beneath the buckled, brittle-boned bridge acutely and audibly anguished, the liquid lines of longevity no longer lingered but vigilantly vanished. Even the wretched, whining weeds in these wicked woods stopped breathing,

succumbing

to

the

schizophrenic

sun

shockingly

sadistic

and

senselessly

seething.

# Bully

Excuse me, *Your Rudeness,* but what did you just now so sarcastically say
under your unbelievably bad breath in such a maniacal, mean-spirited way?
*You wickedly wretched warthog!* You have warbled these words before—
behind my turned torso and every closed, locked, and dead-bolted door.

Did your rapidly receding, rancor-riddled brain ever once care to consider
the hurt that is hurled by your warped words so blatantly and bitingly bitter?
You need to know and forever remember that I will not tolerate or ignore
your viscerally vicious and venomous verbiage I acutely and abidingly abhor.

A foul fate forced us to function like bonded birds of a familiar feather
and fanatically finagled a faux friendship that I futilely fought to weather.
But now, there is noticeably nothing at all that ties me to the appalling you,
except the miserable maelstrom of memories I mournfully can never undo.

You don disguises to detract from the fact that you are wild and wooly,
but they cannot hide that you were born a brazen bitch and belligerent bully.
You're stupid. You're worthless. You're seriously scary and verifiably very
strange, and your large lips and chubby chin are close enough to marry.

Fetid fungus fills the fearsome fissures inside your evil-encased ears,
and if you had the ability to cry, toxic trash would taint your tears.
You're shameless. You're shameful. You're obnoxious. You're hateful.
You're chronically cruel, utterly unfeeling, and unequivocally ungrateful.

Your sin-saturated, slothful soul subsists solely on secrecy and lies,
anger, envy, greed, pride, parasitic pound cakes, and prickly pies
that fester inside flesh-eating fields where filth sleeps seductively among
the wrathful words that disgustingly drip from the tip of your twisted tongue.

Your body does not have a heart, and your soul coldly feels no guilt.
You feed off the pain of those you pursue and wallow in watching them wilt.
Your raucous, reckless, roguish, ruthless, and revoltingly rude tendencies
are regrettably resistant to readily retrievable and rehabilitative remedies.

Your vileness, once a vitriolic veneer, has become a vascularized disease, whose secretions saturate sleazy spaces with the speed of steroids on skis. Your abominable aim is to morbidly maim with your nefariously notched knife, my heavy heart, screaming soul, suffering spirit, and lifeless life.

Your number's up, *you bastardly bully,* so you'd better not hold your breath. Next and last on your terroristic to-do list is a devastating dance with death. You're a notable nobody going nowhere except to hell's hollowed-out hole,

where

the

devil

and

his

battalion

of

bullies

will

forever

torment

your

sadistic

soul.

# Not There

She had always been the first student in the ruinously repressive room,
where she silently sat in her secluded seat inside the ghoulish gloom.
She needfully navigated her netherworldly niche of nerve-numbed nothingness,
rawly riddled with repressed emotions she could not reconcile or express.

She lived her life in fear of death from an illness, injury, or attack,
which is why she, for protection from predation, did choose a seat in the back.
This steadfastly stable, suitably solid, and substantially safeguarded chair
was the only one in which she could sit and hide her debilitating despair.

With a curious quietness, she swiftly slowed her breathless breathing.
After closing her empty eyes, she commenced her inconspicuous grieving.
The classroom's characteristic commotion continued to be caustically chaotic,
as her mind spun threads from shredded thoughts that were primarily psychotic.

The schoolmarm stood in front of the stirred-up students she tensely taught
while the dissidents dished out disobedience as they ferociously fought.
The teacher scribbled something on the blackboard using colorful chalk,
whose seismic screeches signified it had sinister secrets to unlock.

The still student's knotted nightmare had no intention of easing or ending
because she had been sentenced to use her whole life solely spending
time masking and muting every mundane motion and minute sound,
which would ensure she could easily exist without the fear of being found.

Sitting surreally like a stone statue, she seemed too serene to be believed.
The students surrounded by her stationary sedateness were doubtlessly deceived.
She endlessly endured twisted torture that strangled her sickened soul,
whose sacred space was readily replaced by a seismic, scar-savaged hole.

Eccentrically empty of emotion, her eerie eyes became disablingly dry.
Her melancholy mind meaninglessly meandered as she muffled a singular sigh.
She sat stoically, silently, and stilly with her humbled hands perfectly folded
to protect herself from the permanent pain of being severely struck or scolded.

Her fears stemmed from yearning years of needs that had never been met.
She listlessly lived a lusterless life whose lethal legacy had long ago been set.
Drowning in a nebulous nothingness and cataclysmically closed off from herself,
she remained an unopened and unread novel on a shunned, sheltered, sunless shelf.

When the dreadful day came to an end, the students exited the room en masse.
The words on the blackboard disappeared when the eraser made its pass.
The tired teacher tidied up her desk, turned off the lights, and left the room,
and the girl still sat safely and securely in her chair inside the ghoulish gloom.

Alone now with the tormented thoughts of her lamentable life's obliteration,
she dozed in a disturbing daze of doubt, doom, desperation, and damnation.
No one ever noticed her sitting in the room on her chaste, cheerless chair

because

she,

throughout

all

of

her

fear-filled

years,

had

never

once

been

there.

# Six Steps to Somewhere

The supernatural story of the spiral staircase was in secrecy strongly steeped. Suspicion surrounded *the last six steps,* from whose squeaks, scary sagas leaped. The mansion's maids and butlers dared only keep in safeguarded sight those steps beneath the sinister six, which spared them spine-splintering fright.

The sinister steps were solidly sealed with a psychoses-spawning stain and sequestered in a sunless space where they were forever forced to remain. A mad monster malignantly manipulated these macabrely marred six stairs that morphed into malevolent mutants meddling in metaphysical affairs.

The sprawling steps on this serpentine staircase suffered no rebellious resistance, until the time, at *the sinister six steps'* indignant and irreversible insistence, they were hopelessly hindered by hyperventilating haste that harrowingly halted them at a landing beneath a concerning ceiling that was conscientiously vaulted.

At the left of the landing, the six sinister steps staked their creepy claim to a disturbing door above them that deviously delighted in its devilish fame. The deadly door had never been opened, and its entryway had never been seen by the mansion's current residents, their maids, butlers, and pantry queen.

Someone or something had, at some time, the six sinister steps walked and reached the hellishly hungry red door that was both bolted and locked. Someone or something had, at some time, stroked this shuddersome red door stained by someone or something that, at some time, had badly bled.

A century ago, the first maid and butler had, during their enthusiastic employ, ascended and descended the spiral staircase with a sensational sense of joy. They'd never reached the landing that led to the sinister six steps and door because this thought had filled them with fright they'd felt forced not to ignore.

But soon, their eagerness for exciting exploration put their former fears to bed after they received an irresistible invitation to confidently climb without dread the last six steps that scarily led to the death-drenched, dead-bolted door, knowing not what surreptitious surprises for their souls lay silently in store.

Intrigued by their invitation, the maid and butler the spiral staircase walked. They scaled the last six sinister steps leading to the scarlet door, locked. As they tenaciously twisted the gnarly knob of the bleak, blood-bloated door,

they

disturbingly

disappeared

beneath

it

and

were

seen

and

heard

nevermore.

# Rained Out

I lived for the luscious love lavished upon me by the resplendent rain.
The rain romantically refreshed my sad soul, reluctant to relinquish its pain.
Whether the rain's refrains were relaxed or rattled, I refused to run for cover.
The reassuring rain rousingly remained my readily responsive lover.

The rain soothed my splintered spirit and sick, scarred, stagnant soul
with its seductive, succulent drops that with flawless fluidity did roll
into my craving crevices and off every compliant and captivating curve
that lured my lover into unleashing lust that liberally lay in robust reserve.

The rain released my ready randiness with its madly mesmerizing motions
as I moved, moaned, melted, and screamed and succumbed to its commotions.
I dried its divinely dangling droplets with my sweet, sultry, sensitive tongue
and eagerly exposed my exploding emotions as they electrifyingly came undone.

The rain sensed the stimulating situations that brought me to ecstasy's ledge,
where the deliciousness of its drenching drops drove me over the excited edge.
The rain teasingly trickled when its topical tenderness was what I needed
and caressed me each time I playfully panted and profoundly pleaded.

As I signaled my soon-to-surface submission, the rain sped up its undulations,
and I surrendered to the sweet sensations that surpassed my erotic expectations.
My romantic rendezvous with the rambunctious rain rekindled the real reasons
I sought its slippery secretions during the sapless spells of my soulless seasons.

I remained insanely intoxicated by my lover's endlessly energetic expressions
that fueled my fiery feminine fetishes and laundry list of lustful obsessions.
I became significantly sexually stirred at the sight of its seductive display,
which daringly demonstrated its delirious desire for fast and feverish foreplay.

Reading my readiness to be reunited, it wrestled me to the wet weeping ground,
and with sheets of shiversome showers did my petrified person pound.
I was painfully penetrated by its prideful perversion meant to evilly eradicate
my body, mind, soul, and spirit with its humiliating and heartless hate.

Reenergized by its reincarnation as a revenant riddled with rabid rage,
the rain took our love from a romance book to a murder novel's page.
As it vomited vulgarity and vitriol in a violently victimizing way,
the rain cemented my supposition that I had no chance of getting away.

My blatantly bruised and battered body buckled and bitterly bled
onto the once glorious, gorgeous, green grass, now a corrupted shade of red.
From the shuddersome shards of shameful betrayal that the rain did send,
my skin split and exposed my muscles now mangled and unable to bend.

The surreally scary and shattering sounds of my galactic, gruesome groans
manifested themselves in deafening decibels that broke my besieged bones.
To every realm of restorative resuscitation, I was rendered radically resistant
as my body had become instantly, irreverently, and irreversibly nonexistent.

The romantic rain had for a treasured time my responsive regions set free,
but a Luciferian lunacy led my long-time lover to lethally liquidate me.
My nothingness oppressively occupied a spaceless space in a timeless time
within a wicked world that woefully withered without any warning or rhyme.

A lover can torturously turn a tender, touching, and tantalizing gaze
into a horrifically hurtful, hellishly hot, and blistering, billowing blaze
whose hideous heat will burn a horrendously huge and hateful hole

into

its

lover's

unprepared,

unprotected,

and

utterly

unsuspecting

soul.

# The Search

She would not be disturbed on that damp, dreary, and disjointed day.
She categorically could not be found as not a single clue led the way
to her whereabouts in a warped world that worsened her perpetual pain
and chillingly compelled her closer to the creepy clutches of the insane.

One woman wondered if she had wandered into the woods for a walk.
Tantamount to this theory was the town's twittering and tattle talk,
which suggested she was on the shore where she sometimes sought peace
and, from her severe and sustained suffering, seized a short-lived release.

Some surmised she was searching for solace in a space safe for sleeping,
secure with silent serenity from scary strangers who were serially peeping
into her psyche, suspecting that something startling they would find
if they could take a self-guided tour inside her mood-manipulated mind.

As people upon her lonely and lackluster life lamentingly reflected,
their disturbing descriptions depicted her as dangerously disconnected
and, sadly, sidelined from savoring the soothing softness of serenity's face
as she bypassed the beautiful blessings, she was born to never embrace.

Her eerily elusive existence epitomized her quest for quintessential peace,
which magic, mystics, and metaphysics could not help her buy or lease.
Those who loved her were unsuccessful in their attempts to understand
why her hemorrhaging head seemed scarily stuck in the suffocating sand.

Street sleepers and savvy socialites both searched the surf-splashed shore
where they sifted through sand, ceaselessly swept to the sea's salty floor.
After carefully combing the coast for clues, the crowd remained blind
to even the most superficial signs that might make her easier to find.

Her family and friends fiercely fought their fears of her never being found
or discovered years later beneath seashells scattered atop a sand mound.
They were fixated on the fatalistic fact that her life had never bloomed
and possibly disappeared into distressing dormancy prematurely entombed.

Some souls sensed she was seismically sick and in pathetic, permanent pain and uncannily unable to unequivocally unravel, unveil, understand, and explain the caustic content of her complicated emotions clearly corrupted and confused, and on the chilling cusp of a catastrophic collision with a life unlived and unused.

Where she had gone was a private place that was accessible only to her. It was a *secret somewhere* situated inside a bizarrely blinding blur. She had slipped away to a terrifying space where naked nothingness meets pure pain.

She

had

silently,

swiftly,

and

sadly

gone

inescapably

and

irreversibly

insane.

# Mangled Vines

The writhing woodland of wickedness waged its wrath, which was hardwired to taunt and terrorize the terrain within which was torturously quagmired. Vicious vines dangerously dangled and twisted into tensely tangled, noticeably nefarious, gnarly knots that were maliciously and menacingly mangled.

Lurching leaves frighteningly fell from terrifyingly traumatized trees as midnight's mayhemic meddling brought monsters to their nervous knees. Madly manipulated by supernaturally swirling and suddenly sprawling squalls, the lawless leaves danced drunkenly within the frenzied forest walls.

The paranoid pines whimpered and whined in paralyzingly persistent pain as if ardently attempting the absolute attention of a saintly savior to gain. Spastic squirrels sought safe shelter in their wind-woozy woodland beds, fearing the forbidding feelings that hideously haunted their helpless heads.

The melancholy moon mercilessly moaned upon merging with poisonous plumes of gloom that growled inside grisly graveyards grappling with erupting tombs which tempestuously trounced the timid trolls that wearily and woefully wept as they inside corrupted cemeteries like cold cement spine-chillingly slept.

Glowing ghosts groaned above the grumbling ground as it was greedily grabbed by nocturnal, nerve-numbing nettles whose needles nefariously nabbed and calculatingly killed all woodland life that lingered with hopes of revival amid the thicket of trembling trees that relinquished its right to survival.

The raucous rain's rebellion-riddled ranting and repulsively relentless riffs echoed eerily off the craggy, corroded, and catastrophically contorted cliffs. Timorously twittering, terror-troubled tanagers sat on their perches and searched for a perfect and permanent piece of peace that plainly could not be unearthed.

The saturating sheets of restless rain fell furiously into monstrous mountains out of whose malignant mouths fulminated flagrantly formidable fountains. The rain trampled and treacherously tortured fertile fields of flourishing flowers now hideously hushed from the ruthless rush of seriously schizophrenic showers.

With a punishing primeval power that permanently penetrated time and space,
livid lighting struck and severely scarred the black sky's fragile face
and tempestuously twisted the tentacled threads of scary, sterile starkness
into a world of lethally luminous light and deadly debilitating darkness.

Turbulent thunder taunted and frightened the fully fractured and psychotic sky
with vigorously vomiting virulent vibrations that sought to sadistically supply
feral fear following the Luciferian lightning that emulated the essence of electric
evilness on this nightmarish night extraordinarily enigmatic and eccentric.

Ravenous, rain-rattled rabbits raced in hydrophobic hyperventilating haste
toward tenuous, teasing tendrils that tempted their tender tongues with taste.
Bloated black buzzards burst like balls of blistered glass suddenly shattered
as howls of heinous horror throughout this dark, demented forest were scattered.

Gone forever now to nebulous, needful, and netherworldly places
were gnomes that were glaringly gruesome without traces of their faces.
Throngs of trolls singing sorrowful songs with uncanny, unending verses
were tormented, toppled, and transported to toxically tenebrous traverses.

What menacing mystery moves below these desperate, devilish clouds
wickedly watchful within their sanctuary of strange and sinister shrouds?
A wrathful wraith has revealed its revolting, reckless, and ruinous resolution
to disturb, desecrate, and destroy the sacred seeds of humankind's evolution.

Time has been forced to forfeit its finely feathered, nature-nurtured nest,
inside which it had soothingly suckled the breathlessly beautiful breast
of life which, having languished after its last labored and lacerated breath,

has

become

the

eternally

# SCARY

endless
ending
we
darkly
define
as
death.

# Chapter and Verse

Tilting trees twisted within a tapestry that taunted the tenebrous skies,
which were drenched in disemboweled demons with mortal sins for eyes.
Suspiciously swirling leaves were surreptitiously scattered and blown
to disgusting dens that with the devil's dung were dangerously overgrown.

Barren banks bestrewn with broken branches were burrowed into by moles
while the turmoiled topography was tangled with tiny twirling trolls.
Weary, worrisome, woodland weaklings wandered into wilderness spaces
where lightning and thunder tattooed terror onto their traumatized faces.

Blissful brooks, peaceful ponds, lazy lakes, and serene sleepy streams
were clandestinely caught in horrid hooks that savagely split their seams
and penetrated, polluted, and petrified the righteous respectable rivers
that signaled the salty sea's subjugation to substantially seismic shivers.

Mercilessly mangled by morbid madness and fraught with fathomless fear,
the unusually unbalanced universe out of control did alarmingly appear.
The strikingly shrill sounds of substances suddenly bursting and breaking
shocked and sickened the sensitive souls who were screaming and shaking.

Psychoses and savageness surrounded this surreal, spine-splintering scene
that tumbled in tactile turmoil above the grim, groaning, and garishly green
earth perpetually pursued, punishingly pounded, and perilously pulled
by something significantly scary that over this sinister landscape ruled.

This *scary something* smelled of sulfur while it tormented and killed
the humblest and holiest life forms, which now lay silenced and stilled.
From its cursed crust to its crucified core, the earth had been rearranged,
propelling it and its primeval predecessors to places permanently estranged.

Made filthy by fermenting froth forcefully fashioned into flesh-eating fog,
this diabolic dominion was dramatically drowning in a brooding bacterial bog.
The devil, with his horrifying hideousness, sadistically sought to evilly expose
the most terrifying tips of the thorniest thorns on the bleakest and blackest rose.

The soft, sweet, sacred, and soothing sounds of soul-saving serenity blasphemously became the vengeful voice of an evil-centered entity that usurped unauthorized ownership of this once happy and holy space now sickeningly saturated with mortal sin that signaled its slip from grace.

Over serrated, steel, sanguinary knives horrified humans howled and hovered as the devil delectably dismembered them, creating crinkle-cut clumps covered in blood and then halted his hideous hacking to begin hastily chasing after

the

next

victims

waiting

inside

this

catastrophically

chilling

chapter.

# Victorian Heat

The venerable, vine-covered, Victorian mansion had recently been bought by a wondrously wealthy woman who had desperately dreamed of and sought the breathless beauty, gilded grandeur, and enchantingly elegant expanse that would with its lustrous lure of luxury this woman eternally entrance.

She was a middle-aged woman who had decided never to marry because she believed that matrimony would her bohemian backbone bury. Marriage would dismally destroy her with its deluge of debilitating demands—the ones that a mundane married life miserably and mindlessly commands.

She blossomed into a woman blissfully blessed and considerably content and rapturously relieved, knowing that she would celebrate and not lament the fact that she had no partner with whom she had been sentenced to share this magical and majestic mansion where *one person* truly trumped *a pair*.

This Victorian house's spacious suites were saturated with secret places where she sought a sanctuary when the significantly schizophrenic paces of her chokingly choreographed life were quite calamitously convoluted, making these specially situated, soothing spaces for her much better suited.

But the scorching, stalking, summer sun strove to make her sweat and suffer, and not even a benevolent, blithesome breeze became a beneficial buffer between the wilted woman and the heat that caused her to feel faint and did her love and longing for the summer months severely taint.

The sun's steaming, suffocating stimulation did not stymie her dream of seclusion inside this sanctum situated next to a sleepy stream that fearlessly and fluidly flowed in fathomless, free-spirited directions and took detours that could not dodge death's disordered intersections.

In a valley vibrant with vegetation, the Victorian house had been built in the year 1890, when a noble family did wickedly wilt because it had been sadistically sentenced the seething, summer season to bear until the father, fraught with futility, fought off the fiendish air.

# Barbara Eck Tosi

The father was a wealthy, willful, and worrisomely wrongheaded man. He spent a fortune furnishing his family with many a fancy floor fan. The fans forced fiery air to fly in a fashion that was fearsomely frenetic, which proved they were undeniably useless and exceptionally eccentric.

The feverish fortress filled with fancy floor fans unable to render relief had caused the frustrated father and his family to formulate the belief that only a cold spell could categorically clear the chronically comatose circulation that prompted their painful pulmonary problems and duels with dehydration.

Every doomed day the outside temperature had continued its significant rise, and its ill effects had not caused the *irascible incompatibles* any surprise. Their overtly overheated, tempestuous tempers had freely and frighteningly flared as they in muggy, maniacal misery at one another had scarily stared.

One overpoweringly oppressive afternoon, the father had abruptly appeared before his flummoxed family with his face and neck severely seared. The hostilely hot and hissing sun had shown no soul-saving sign of freeing this frazzled family from its dangerously deranged and dying vine.

The man's wife and seven children had been uncomfortably sitting in the parlor with their lifeless lips parted and teeth grotesquely gritting. Tormented for too long by torrid temperatures that tested and taxed their souls, they crouched on couches that collected sweat dripping from their bodies' holes.

In a despicable deed of desperation, the father, a heavy hatchet, took into the parlor where he presented his family with a petrifying look. Oblivious to those he loved most on the exponentially evaporating earth, he hastily to a hellacious hatefulness gave live, lethal, and evil birth.

He brutally beheaded his fevered family with the swift, savage motions of a heathen high on hallucinogens and poison-possessing potions. With a powerful pistol previously protected behind a well-hidden shelf, he, with one bullet through the head, killed his demonic and demented self.

# SCARY

Lying next to the heads and bodies of his family disturbingly deceased,
he, along with them, had been frighteningly but fortunately released
from the summer sun's sinisterly scorching, suffocating, and sulfuric heat,
which systematically did their screaming spirits deliberately defeat.

Substantially saturated with salty sweat that she could not combat,
the woman inside the pulseless parlor on a chair in sogginess sat.
As she tried to relax, she suddenly, out of the corner of her right eye,
spotted a Victorian gentleman sporting a smile that was wickedly wry.

He sneakily and slyly took a seat on a stiff, stuffed, sun-scarred chair
that had been frayed from fabric fatigue caused by frequent wear.
The venturous visitor vacated his seat and vanished from earthly view,
which alarmed the anxious woman who assumed her astigmatism was askew.

But the stranger surfaced once again and stood bizarrely behind her chair,
holding high his hellish hatchet in the hatefully heavy asphyxiating air.
He heartlessly hacked off her humidity-harassed head to hijack her hefty sweat.
He blindly believed this atrocious action would forever put her in his debt.

The hatchet-happy hero who had put a halt to her headstrong hyperhidrosis
was the 1890s man who had beheaded his family while suffering from psychosis.
After securing the woman's head and body in a seamlessly secret space,
the hot-headed heliophobe hibernated inside his haunted hiding place.

There the morbid megalomaniac for a new owner did wickedly wait
because it was that person's sweaty soul, he did so anxiously anticipate.
Strategically situated at his secluded station, far from the sick, savage sun,

the

hellspawn

held

high
his
head-hacking
hatchet
from
which
no
new
owner
could
run.

# A Life in Pieces

As she sifted through a stack of old family clothing situated on her kitchen table, the sweet soulful mother and wise, wonderful wife was most amazingly able to visualize the pile as quilted pieces arranged like a jigsaw puzzle while her feline's furry face against the narrow nape of her neck did nuzzle.

From many years of use, the cherished clothes had become faded and torn, but long ago, they did the mother's family members fashionably adorn. Although they now lay limp and lifeless within the fastidiously folded stack, her recollections of them resurrected the richness they had reveled in years back.

A young child's cheerful Christmas dress that showcased its satin sash lay tenderly on the very top of the solidly sweet and sacred stash of her close-knit family's clothes, which she had purchased and protected during the blessed and bountiful years upon which she now reflected.

Beneath this pretty party dress, a plain petticoat adorably appeared. It was besmirched with brown stains suggesting that it had been seared by an irate, irreverent iron whose tetchy temperature had abruptly ascended and seriously scorched the petticoat while it was unintentionally unattended.

Below these angelic articles of clothing an aged apron the woman spotted. It was yarrow yellow in color and with white, round, raised spots dotted. Fortifying its flawed and fragile fabric that was now thoroughly threadbare were memories of the many meals she with her motherly love did prepare.

Beneath her yellow, dotted Swiss apron was a pretty pastel-pink bonnet more poetic even in its paleness than Shakespeare's eighteenth sonnet. Her dutiful daughter had donned the bonnet after much maternal persuasion and then willingly worn it for every frill-less and fancy family occasion.

The bonnet brought forth magical memories from many Thanksgivings back when the merciful mother had picked out potatoes from a bulging burlap sack. She'd boiled and mashed them inside a pot and then placed them on a rack inside her old-fashioned oven where they for warmth would never lack.

When the holiday table had been specially set in preparation for food to serve, she filled her grandmother's fine china bowl that she had held in reserve with piping hot mashed potatoes, which she dolloped with pats of butter as she continued inside her quaint kitchen to cook, bake, and joyfully putter.

She privately prayed that her family would always know and eternally feel the unconditional and limitless love that she in her huge heart did seal. She wished for them to wallow in the warmth of her soul's solid white light when desperate days become many a dismally dark and depressing night.

After the emotional hours elapsed, the woman grew weak and weary. As she touched the tender tears that had turned her beautiful blue eyes bleary, she pondered the paths her family had pursued in both sunshine and rain and passageways punctuated with periods of pure joy and pulsating pain.

After transferring the tower of timeless threads to a properly protected place, she glowed from God's glistening gift of glorious and generous grace. Mellowed by her many meaningful memories, she readied herself for bed and dreamed about this most blessed day and the blessed days ahead.

The next morning she gathered the garments and cut them into many a piece and produced a patchwork quilt that long after her death would never cease to fill her family with faith, hope, love, and memories that would always abide

inside

this

quilt

where

her

selfless

spirit
for
all
time
would
rightfully
reside.

# Serenity

Sweetly serene this dreamy day seemed with its penetrating, pastoral pureness that deliriously dozed inside its delicately dappled and delightful demureness. The day remained remarkably restful as it effortlessly and uniquely unfolded into a tapestry of treasured timelessness that from magic and mystery was molded.

Tall trees lavishly laden with lusciously lithesome and liberated leaves buried their breathlessly beautiful branches inside the blissful bucolic breeze. Softly silhouetted by a surreally silken and soothingly somnambulant sky, the trees transparently transcended tranquility as the delicious day danced by.

The perfectly poised and polished patches of mossy green meadow grass shimmered with the scintillating sun's each placid and purposeless pass. Creamy cumulous clouds caressed and cushioned the soulfully sedated sky, fascinated by their freely unfurling forms as they peacefully passed by.

The clouds continuously and captivatingly configured their shifting shapes, which drifted like daydreams above the smoothly sculpted and scenic scapes that Mother Nature, with her amazing, alluring, and authentically artistic flair, creatively crafted out of her sacred stores of sun, soil, wind, water, and air.

Lovely lavender lounged on the lazy land's lap, and sweet alyssum slept near nested niches of narcoleptic narcissus that were notoriously adept at napping after nature's nimble nudging did so delicately direct when their chronically confused circadian rhythms, did their sleep cycles upset.

Lady slippers snuggled inside silken seclusion that in softness was dipped as they sleepily into spun-sugar slumber spontaneously and splendidly slipped. The acquiescent afternoon arrived without attracting any arresting attention, and the ethereal evening that was yet to come was given no mind or mention.

The towering trees' limber leaves settled below the swiftly sinking sun, and the drifting canopy of carefree clouds delicately came undone. Serenity saturated the silent stillness on this sublimely simple day.

This

scene

was

kissed

with

beautiful

bliss,

and

only

beautiful

bliss

would

stay.

# Personality Plus

The silver shadows had scarily stalked the girl since she was quite small. The first shadow made its appearance after she suffered her monstrous fall from a wide, warped, weathered windowsill inside a bleak and baneful attic where evil exploited its electric energy through encounters eerie and erratic.

The girl's mother sadly was not at home when the accident had occurred, but immediately after she of her child's mysterious misfortune heard, she directly to her distraught, disordered, and damaged daughter returned, convinced that this catastrophe's cause must very quickly be discerned.

The child's nanny told the mortified mother that it had rained that day while the girl on the attic's open window's sill had been pleasantly at play. She had suddenly slipped on the slick window ledge and had fallen into the air and landed on thick and thorny hedges—a painful bed she could barely bear.

The hellish hedges with horrendous hazardousness were forthrightly fraught. They halted, however, a more horrifying fall by having had the girl caught, rescuing her from a rendezvous with the wretched, rock-riddled ground and preventing her and definitive death from becoming bloodcurdlingly bound.

But the particularly prickly thorns did pierce and penetrate her body so severely, that since the time of that terrifying tumble, she was destined to be yearly seen by the family physician who never in his life could have imagined seeing scars any scarier than the shuddersome ones he on her examined.

Following her freakish, fateful fall, the child had been fearfully followed by a sinister, silver shadow that coldly captured and stealthily swallowed the sense of solid security that had once provided her with protection from the spooky spirits and demented demons that deviously dodged detection.

The startling shadow surreptitiously swelled and became dangerously defiant, goading the gorgonized girl to be on her *scare meter* relentlessly reliant. The slinky shadow maliciously multiplied and with fiendish ferociousness formed a silver sea of psychotic shadows that within her psyche savagely stormed.

# Barbara Eck Tosi

The girl became radically repulsed whenever her bruised brain would swell from memories of that disastrous day that hopelessly hurled her into hell. Her toxic thoughts caused the shady shadows to morbidly multiply in number. Twelve shadows now derisively disrupted her day and sabotaged her slumber.

Tormented by time, each spooky shadow waited its turn to emphatically express the malignant mayhem that cruelly caused it into maniacal madness to digress. Fifteen strangely subversive shadows now in front of her aggressively appeared and flaunted their freakish fixation with fueling everything that she feared.

After the creepy conclusion of this unexpected and unsettling unveiling, the shadows signaled their spite-slimed sadness by then boldly bewailing the fact that only one at a time could take command and brazenly be the pursuer of the girl whose sidelined shadows steeped in their disharmony.

The shadows showcased their slyness by settling into shiversome shapes that grew into grisly grotesqueness generating ghoulish gossamer capes. Mounds of mist mockingly mimicked a malleable mountain range that, with madness back into malicious monsters, did chillingly change.

The shrouded shapes had, through their paranormal powers of coercion, convinced one another to blatantly become a psychotically septic version of the hellishly hounded girl who, when her macabre memories did rage, was required to respond to their requests for recognition on center stage.

These vaporous versions of the girl would vanish and then wishfully wait like vultures for their otherworldly opportunity to ostentatiously demonstrate their appointments by an aberrant authority to authenticate the girl's life by simulating her scarred sensibilities and superabundance of senseless strife.

The girl told her mother that she recalled at one time being hospitalized after the abysmal accident that had rendered her troublesomely traumatized. But due to the severity of the significant suffering she had sadly sustained, her storehouse of scary specifics had been stripped from her battered brain.

Years later, the guarded girl and her mother into the abhorrent attic walked and about the girl's formidable fall tenebrously and twitchily talked. A rabid rainstorm rapidly ravaged the weathered window's wide-open sill, and the suspicion-stricken, shock-saturated girl stood stiffly and seriously still.

"Mother, I remember every diabolic detail of that dreadfully disturbing day. Our ne'er-do-well nanny nibbled on her nails while I on the window's sill did play. Her disconnected demeanor demonstrated her desire for the dreary attic to leave, but I strongly sensed she had more than handkerchiefs up her sinister sleeve.

"When her shuddersome stare struck my shivering senses, I shrilly screamed. She suddenly snapped and, with a sadistically specific savagery, seemed to morph even more into a maniacal and nightmarishly negligent nanny by spontaneously and severely spanking my small, sweet, fragile fanny.

"She pertinaciously pushed me off the worryingly waterlogged window ledge and wickedly watched me as I frightfully fell onto a threatening hedge. Paralyzed with palpably piercing pain and fraught with fathomless fears, I winced as I looked toward the window and witnessed her teasing tears."

Upon hearing this hideously horrific story, the mother, in a manner coy, swiftly summoned the neglectful nanny who was still in the family's employ. The furious mother's formidable fists pounded the foul fiend's face while delivering a disdainful diatribe describing her as a depraved disgrace.

After tightly tying up the nanny, the mother immediately called the police and informed them that she had a crazed criminal to readily release into their custody to be locked up for the remainder of her lunatic life because she had caused her cherished child such cruel and catastrophic strife.

The police arrived at the shocking scene and hauled the nasty nanny away, and padlocked her inside a pitiful prison where she was doomed to die one day. Her pathetic public pleas for mercy proved to be particularly persistent, but soon, any news of the notorious nanny remained noticeably nonexistent.

Systemically scarred and hellaciously haunted by the feral, ferocious fears that perpetually persisted and plagued her through her pathetically painful years, the now grown-up girl seeking a safe sanctuary settled into an appealing abode and miraculously managed *her overtly obtrusive others* to ultimately unload.

Upon being admirably and aptly accepted, she attended an Ivy League college where she studied and systematically stored a comprehensive knowledge of the fundamental functions, footling flaws, and failures of the human mind that four fruitful years of focused fortitude allowed her to fascinatingly find.

During the girl's final semester, she and her close classmates were required to collectively convene at a mental institution that was in lunacy madly mired. Of this secluded, shuttered state hospital, the group was sickeningly afraid, but this trip was necessary for them to receive a graduation-worthy grade.

By their college professor and a sanitarium psychiatrist, they were each escorted to the freakish facility's forbidding fifth floor, which featured an absurdly assorted unhingement of unpredictably unstable patients who, quite crazy and embittered, were the most dangerously disordered of all the building's residents considered.

The stupefied students walked past whining walls on the feared fifth floor while armed guards stood outside each disturbingly doom-drenched door in case any crazed, confrontational patients with insatiable insanity would strive to sabotage the safety of every spooked student that they could.

The collegians were required to document their insightful interpretations of the paranoid patients' otherworldly outbursts and hellish hallucinations. The copious and comprehensive notes that the conscientious class took would later be carefully compiled into a chillingly compelling book.

As the class cautiously approached the final room on the fifth floor, the girl sensed something shocking behind the room's dead-bolted door. The guard uneasily unlocked it, and the group grudgingly gathered inside, whereupon the petrified girl's psyche into pulsating panic did slide.

She readily recognized the wicked woman who was chained to the bed as well as the fifteen silver shadows that filled her head with dread. "You're my fiendish former nanny who is now flooding my field of vision! Why are you here," she shrilly screamed, "and not in the state prison?"

The psychiatrist informed the girl that the woman had previously been a prisoner but was now in a lifetime lockdown in her room within this insane institution where select staff was trained but ultimately unable to put the brakes on her bizarre behavior, which was way beyond unstable.

"Here," he noted, "her demons dimmed those she had displayed in prison. She functioned like a feral fruitcake in the throes of thermonuclear fission. Her explosive episodes erupted erratically and elicited forbidding fear, and that is the resounding reason she must until her death remain here.

"Because she attempted from her room's rain-racked windowsill to jump, she has been mandated upon her mattress to lie in a submissive slump. Her hands and feet are punitively pinioned to the pointed posts on her bed, and a huge harness hanging from the headboard holds up her neck and head.

"Her empty eyes remain fixated on the cosmetically-challenged ceiling—particularly its patches of old paint that are constantly cracking and peeling. This psychotic patient has proven that she can a plethora of people scare. Based on this fact, one beyond-brave aide is solely responsible for her care.

"She exists in this revolting room whose only window has been barred and whose locked and bolted door is monitored by a seasoned security guard. Never again will she be a witness to the world's delightful dichotomy

because

I,

on

her

brain,

many

years

ago,

performed

a

prefrontal

lobotomy."

# The Purple Door

The entire earth abruptly awoke to a suspicious, suffocating smoke that lined the laboring lungs of the living who were left to cough and choke. The slashed sky savagely separated into segments of shards and shreds that portended a day of disturbing doom that even death itself dreads.

Swelling swirls of septic shock spiraled their sordid and sadistic way into the scarred skin of spineless sky that scattered its asymmetrical array of hallucinogenic hues that sighed and sobbed in surreal, supersaturated sadness that painfully penetrated this maniacally macabre and multimottled madness.

A plethora of purple permeated a palette amazingly and alarmingly akin to both royal and religious garments and mortifying mortal sin. The purpleness was a blend of the beautifully blessed and heinously horrific that deftly displayed a disordered dichotomy twixt the demonic and pontific.

A particularly pungent, offensive odor, the hideous haze hauntingly assumed one that was revoltingly reminiscent of insufferable incense perversely perfumed. The peculiarly purple, strangely strangulated sky calculatingly continued to be a supernatural symbol of gloating genius and irreversible insanity.

Just as the sea's whining waves and sandy shoreline are serially parted, the purple sky repetitively redivided, sustaining the splitting it had started. It restlessly revealed its amethyst soul's caustically cold and contorted core, which crashed to earth and gave live birth to a most perplexing purple door.

The purple door posed as a perfect partition between earth's known places and the cosmos' collection of cleverly concealed and curiously cryptic spaces. The door made of petrified purple wood demonstrably stood between the earth and tame or terrifying terrain never before by humankind seen.

The simple word *enter* was plainly printed upon the purple door's front. This interesting invitation made it effortless for those who might want to follow the illogical instruction and find themselves on the other side of this permanently purple door, desperate to unveil what it did hide.

Just below the single word *enter,* there appeared another noteworthy word that was frantically filled with the uneasy urgency of a crazed, cat-stalked bird. The word *now* perfectly positioned itself on the door's palpable purpleness announcing admittance to an audacious adventure, not one person should miss.

Wary watchers were fanatically fixated on this prodding purple door whose imperative words *enter now* did instantly and impatiently implore them to open without any twinges of toxically tormented tension the purple door and daringly discover a distant delphic dimension.

An agonizing hour of absurd anxiousness elapsed without anyone trying to open the purple door and begin peering, poking, and prying into a potentially perilous place brought to life on an unknown date—a place waiting for persons to enter without knowing their ultimate fate.

An intentional intervention interrupted this idiosyncratic illusion causing the petulant purple sky to shed its lavender-laced confusion. No longer was it the fractured, fragmented, and supernaturally struck space that had been the victim of forces that had frightfully filleted its face.

The purple sky backscattered inside a background of bachelor-button blue, and the smoke was suddenly smothered and swiftly vanished from view. The purple door determinedly remained in its authoritatively appointed place and diligently dominated its deliberately designated and alluringly anointed space.

The words *enter now* disappeared from the door and would never again be read. They were replaced with eleven others that resolutely remained in their stead. These eleven words taunted the townspeople who at them did more than glance: "Your fearfulness has fatefully forced you to forfeit your only chance!"

Detrimentally disturbed, deeply demoralized, disenchanted, and disjointed, the dubious dare dodgers descended into despair devastatingly disappointed because the mystery that lamentably lay behind the unpenetrated purple door would

remorsefully

remain

just

that

for

the

fabled

future

of

forevermore.

# Chemistry 101

I was chemically challenged, scientifically sick, and sorely sleep-deprived when the dreaded day of my college chemistry final had finally arrived. I reluctantly reached for my cluster of keys and departed my dark dorm room as visions of beakers and Bunsen burners in my boggled brain did loom.

I tried to titrate my meandering mind's triple-pointed and tenuous traction to create a hypothetically helpful, pipettely perfect chemical reaction that would through osmosis occur between me and this excruciating exam for which I for many weeks had allowed myself to conscientiously cram.

My stellar scholastic standing in this celebrated college could quickly fade if I, on this final chemistry exam, did not receive a gold-gilded grade. After this my swan song semester, I longingly looked forward to getting the demonstrably deserved degree that I for four years had spent sweating.

I augustly admit that of my grade point average, I was profoundly proud, but this challenging chemistry final held a cold and creepy carbon cloud over my helium-filled head and this doom-distilled, density-drenched day, causing an acute anxiety absorbance that I was unable to diffuse or delay.

Chemistry, for me, was a stubborn subject that was lethally left-brained. It direly deionized my durability and rendered my dainty dipoles drained. Its repulsive rigidness and deadly dullness left me absolutely abhorring every cryptic chemical compound my mind continued compulsively storing.

One cold concept I attempted to master was the proverbial periodic table which I at certain times and with adequate aeration was somewhat able to periodically ponder, partially perceive, and painstakingly recall as I was sure that questions about it on the final exam would fall.

My chemistry professor dwelled deep inside his chemically cluttered mind, which was seismically sad because he could not a filtrated formula find that would adequately allow him to deftly depolarize and reactively relate to his students who, for his aerobically autoclaved attention, did wait.

## Barbara Eck Tosi

They never saw his eyes, nose, ears, and other pertinent personal features—all of which distinctly different appeared on the faces of their other teachers. During all limiting reagent lectures, his buffered back to them was turned, which is why he the non-electrolytic nickname *"Professor No Face"* earned.

During his limp lecture on liquefaction, his selenium-synthesized sweater covered his convex chemistry commentary, which he followed to the letter. With the blackboard wholly hidden, the spectator ion students could not see his notes until the end of the class when he in the room would no longer be.

Once he was gone, we could confirm that his lithium-laden, lone pair lecture was tinctured with a thermonuclear and theoretically yielded texture as the beryllium-bonded blackboard volatile, vulcanized, and vainly vibrant spilled forth his node-worthy notes like rushing water from a fire hydrant.

I entered the electrically energized room where quarks of questions waited for all who were seated, radioactively ready, and catalytically congregated. With the exothermic exams (and some students) completely passed out, I put pi-bonded pen to polymer paper to temper my triple-bonded doubt.

With his surfactant back to us, the polyatomic professor suddenly turned, and that is when we in salifiable, supersaturated shock literally learned that his disease of electron-paired repulsion was the reason he never faced our class as his nuclear-fissioned features had been electrochemically erased.

"From a cathodically charged chemistry catastrophe, I lost both of my eyes as well as my nose and ears," he announced with stoichiometric surprise. "My soft surface tension scars are a centrifuged color of free-radical red. My years as a college chemistry professor are hereby denatured and dead.

"You will not receive any academic credits for this colloidally cursed class, and that's not because I have a cooling curve that is combustible and crass. I cannot see, so I've naturally never seen the lackluster, lousy lot of you in this lecture hall hidden within a building protected from public view.

"A two-eyed Pauli principled professor will teach the class this coming term. You must meet with this vaporized man and make your polarized plans firm. You will require those compulsory credits to receive your college degree

and

from

me

and

Chemistry

101

to

be

completely

compound

free."

# Seriously Serial

National TV broadcasters were the burdened bearers of nightmarish news since the first dead woman was spotted without her clothes and shoes. Another brutalized body had been by FBI agents recently recovered after a hiker inside deep woods had her bare body disturbingly discovered.

The FBI suspected a serial killer had committed these two crazed crimes. Their current crime candidate had come close to killing his wife a few times. Pinning down this potential perpetrator presently proved not to be possible as his absence of acquaintances made learning his location implicitly illogical.

One day when her husband was at work, the woman left and never came back. When her spouse realized she was gone for good, he wanted all women to attack. His wrathful reaction resulted in a ruthlessness that monopolized his mind as he went on the warpath watching for women to witness his hatred unwind.

He ferreted out females who realistically resembled his renegade, reprobate wife. When such a *she* was in his sights, he seized her and snuffed out her life. He tortured his tantalizing trophies and targeted them for a devilish demise because it merits mentioning again: they mirrored his wife, whom he did despise.

A villainous variety of maniacal methods for their monstrous murders he chose because he claimed that his constantly changing, considerably confusing MOs would further complicate the challenging components of the FBI's frantic search and leave them hanging in a huge head-scratching and straw-grasping group lurch.

The man was enormously empowered by these evil events he eerily enjoyed knowing that the fathomlessly frightening formats he energetically employed to terrifyingly torment and twistedly terminate each woman he would pick would suitably satisfy his savage sadism so shockingly and shiveringly sick.

To circumvent capture and cruel confinement, he changed his notorious name. He hoped this would help him to hide behind his flagrantly flagitious fame. He appreciably altered his anatomical appearance so that no one could see that *his* face was the *killer's* face blatantly broadcast on national TV.

# Barbara Eck Tosi

Dozens of women had disgustingly died at the serial killer's heinous hand. After he murdered each victim, he mercilessly, *one more* victim did demand. His compulsive craving for cryptic killing did increasingly intensify, as did the bloodthirsty, barbaric brutality he used to make his victims die.

Not permitting its painstaking perseverance and precious progress to lose, the FBI aimed its astute attention on accumulating any careless clues that the sociopathic serial slayer may have sloppily left behind as he cautiously crisscrossed the country his categorical concealment to find.

One December morning, a sudden snowstorm suppressed his slaughtering spree. Forced to stay inside, he flashed back to Christmases filled with frivolity and homemade holiday cookies so sensationally satisfying and sweet he was compelled to quell his cravings with a terrifically tantalizing treat.

He spotted a sack of sugar showcasing a cherished Christmas cookie recipe whose simple specifications suddenly suspended his search for something sugary. He gathered the gratifying goods and gear that were recognizably required to create these cookies that, when cooled, would be with festive frosting attired.

Sadly the same simple sack of sugar that had surprisingly supplied him with a reliable recipe for Christmas cookies was seriously small and slim. The distressing discovery that his sole sugar supply was lamentably low caused this crazed killer to confront an unexpected and unsettling blow.

He had believed he could bake his cookies without any cause for pause, but his significant sugar shortfall led him to lock his jutting jaws. He felt that perhaps a friendly knock on his next-door neighbor's front door would be the surest and speediest strategy for supplemental sugar to implore.

This troubling twist threw threatening turbulence into his baking plans, so in his pantry, he pinpointed a pail that was posing as one of his pans. His pain over the prospect of meeting his neighbor spiraled into seismic shock, but with his plan in place and pail poised, he, upon his neighbor's door, did knock.

# SCARY

After a warm woman welcomed him, the mentally misaligned man did give her the information that he in the house next door to her did live. He said he was seeking to solicit some sugar that he wished to borrow, promising that if she had sugar to share, he would replace it on the morrow.

Before this sweet soul sans suspicion had the chance to speak one word, the stealthy serial slayer shrilly shouted, "This is absolutely absurd! You look exactly like my wife!" Then he brandished a nightmarish knife

and

suddenly

and

savagely

stabbed

her

until

he

subsequently

stilled

her

life.

# Last-Chance Bridge

Filbert was a beautifully behaved boy, and his innocence was well known. During his socially skittish days, however, he had become pitifully prone to foolishly falling for his faux friends' relentless ridicule and killer kidding and their ridiculous, radical requests for him to do their bloodsucking bidding.

His shyness squared with his special soul, soft spirit, and scintillating smile—a combination that could coax a captured criminal to confess before his trial. Although this exceptionally eccentric example is outlandishly outrageous, it clearly clarifies why the boy's coy charm was considerably efficacious.

Over time Filbert's phony friends' connivance convinced him to partake in their devilish deeds, which were done for their shamefully selfish sake. They torturously teased him and thrust him into turmoil that they thought would brilliantly bring them the addictive attention they so sordidly sought.

Whenever faithful, fun-loving Filbert was faced with any choices to make, he copycatted the choices of his crusty chums so he would not break his pattern of playing a pathetic part in their childishly capricious charades that characterized him as a crackbrained clown in their prideful, public parades.

They persistently pointed out to Filbert that he was generous and good-hearted and a pertinent part of the friendship fraternity they had many years ago started. They fiendishly focused on injuring his innocence from the time he was younger and subjected him to their sadistic strategies to satisfy their hedonistic hunger.

They appallingly appeased their aberrant appetite by perniciously poking fun at flinching, floundering Filbert, who lacked the soul-saving sense to run away from them because if he did, they would lick their lying lips and laugh. Filbert suffered their sick savagery as they were the seeds, and he was the chaff.

For his futilely feral friends' foolish flimflam, the fine Filbert forever fell because the sweet shyness with which he was born made him much too swell of a mate to mistrust the mercurial motives of this callously corrupted club. Unfortunately for Filbert, the faithful follower, therein lay the ruinous rub.

# Barbara Eck Tosi

Once when Filbert had the flu, his friends said he'd had a nervous breakdown. Filbert's classmates repeated the rumor and spread it throughout the town. People pictured Filbert with the patients who in the insane asylum did stay. When he showed up at school one day, the students screamed and scurried away.

Faithful Filbert tolerated that dreadfully dismal and demoralizing day, and even after suffering the horrible humiliation, he was still unable to stay away from the familiar, foul, false friends who compulsively counted on him to conveniently carry out their every wily and wretchedly wicked whim.

Another time the phony friendship fraternity followed Filbert to his home. While Filbert prepared their lunch, they searched his clothes closet with a comb. They unveiled an unbelievably ugly outfit and then convinced Filbert to wear the eccentric ensemble to school the next day, where he'd be deliciously debonair.

They hinted that he'd be a hugely hip hunk in these cool and classy clothes and that his preeminent presence would pressure all the girls to betray their beaus. They stated that his sensational sightliness would spark a spectacular stir inside the school where shifts in style like his did shockingly seldom occur.

Notwithstanding the nervous breakdown betrayal, he believed what they had said. The very next morning, Filbert confidently laid the clownish clothes upon his bed and spryly sported them to school, feeling that he would fuel a fashion fever. After enduring endless embarrassment, in this fever, he was no longer a believer.

Filbert's false "friends" had brainwashed him into being belittled like this. He was pitifully and painfully programmed a perfect prospect never to miss to flatter his faux, feckless friends, for whom he would walk to the very ends of the earth and then back again to further his future as their friends.

Filbert was trapped inside their thorny trenches of time-tested tricks. He bought into their barbaric behavior that never ceased him to transfix. His friends' endless enjoyment of evil continued to exist and escalate the more the needy, nonchalant Filbert naively nibbled at their baleful bait.

On the last day of school, Filbert received a nebulous note from Jewel. Jewel was a stunning student who attended classes at Filbert's school. Although he and Jewel had never met, he delighted in her from a distance and was mesmerized by her message immersed in intoxicating insistence.

"My fondest Filbert, I beseech you to meet me this evening if you can," were the wondrous words with which Jewel's nerve-numbing note began. "I will anticipate your arrival at Last-Chance Bridge at the precise time of eight. I heartily hope we will see each other then. Please be there and don't be late!"

After this final day of school had ended, flustered Filbert hustled to his house, and himself and his handsome clothes in his father's cologne did douse. To no one did he mention the note that Jewel to him had written, nor did he let on that he, over her, was spellbindingly smitten.

Before leaving, Filbert fetched a gun hidden behind an heirloom hutch. He required it to restrain the roaming rattlesnakes, ruffians, and such that might initiate intimidation and interfere with this impending interlude and nefariously negate the first night of many with Jewel to be accrued.

Filbert placed the gun inside its holster and hid the duo from public view. If anything or anyone perturbed his path, he patently knew what to do. He told his mother he would be at a party to celebrate the school year's end. He felt like a fraud because his parting words to her were ones of pure pretend.

Alone now, Filbert comprehensively contemplated Jewel's curiously cryptic note. He suddenly became awkwardly aware of a large lump lodged in his throat. He pondered the purpose of Jewel's invitation to meet with her and talk at this offbeat hour on this backwoods bridge where scary spirits loved to walk.

Filbert could not remember a time in his life when he'd been as excited as he was at this magical moment after having been by Jewel politely invited to the Last-Chance Bridge for this most mysterious and mystifying meeting, the thought of which caused his hyper heart to bulge from beyond-belief beating.

After walking two miles, he reached Last-Chance Bridge precisely at eight.
Upon searching and seeing no sign of Jewel, Filbert proceeded to patiently wait.
He passed the torturous time by silently sitting upon a reassuring rock
as the cruel clock tensely ticked, and it quickly became nine o'clock.

As the miserable minutes moved on, Filbert's watch revealed it was nine-thirty.
His psyche snapped as he knew this meeting was just another mean and dirty
trick his faux friends, whom he now abhorred, had once again pulled—
yet another twisted time he had been by them so humiliatingly fooled.

As he rose from the rock, he suddenly heard vaulting voices and lilting laughter.
His suspicion became a surety that these feckless fiends had directed this disaster.
"You fell for it, Filbert," the viciously venomous villains were sarcastically saying.
"Jewel isn't coming. She doesn't know you exist. We were just, you know, playing!

"We smelled your big-boy cologne a mile behind you on this desolate road.
You look so silly and super stupid standing there like a tuxedoed toad.
Go home to your mommy so she can kiss your horribly hoodwinked head
and read you your favorite fairy tale and tuck you into your little-boy bed."

Filbert ragingly reached into his holster and pulled out his guarded gun.
As he pointed it at them, they shouted shrilly, "We were only having fun!"
They pleaded with Filbert to put down the weapon and hear their explanation.
When he didn't, they jumped into the deep dark river without any hesitation.

Filbert howled hysterically as he witnessed the frauds furiously flailing about.
None of them knew how to swim and choked as they struggled to shout.
As the slimy sleazeballs simultaneously sank in a frantically futile fit,
Filbert cried, "*You barbaric bunch of bastardly brutes finally fell for it!*

*"You're a brotherhood of bottom-feeding, backboneless sons of bitches.*
Never again will I follow your lethal lead and scratch your imbecilic itches.
Why did you jump, you junkyard jerks? I was just—you know, having fun.

The

weapon

I

waved

at

you

whimpering

wussies

was

a

worthless

wannabe

gun!”

# Delicious Dismemberment

She beamed like a bouquet of bursting buttercups the moment she was born. Her intoxicating iridescence, however, was sorely subject to shameful scorn that severely scarred, permanently pitted, and fully fractured her fragile face. Throughout her lifeless lifetime, she could never these fatal flaws erase.

Her turbulent torment tragically transformed into a ton of solidified cement that formidably fell upon her fragileness and induced an irreversible indent. Her see-through skin seeped with a septic stench that was sickeningly akin to past-their-prime parsnips pungently putrefying in a parasitic produce bin.

Fermenting fissures cruelly colonized her corruptly corroded cheeks, which were drier than the dusty dirt in desiccated and decaying creeks. Her nearly nonexistent nose nurtured a notion that a freakishly fat someone or something had forced it into a frightful future of being flat.

Since the disastrously distressing dawn of her disabling, dysfunctional days, disordered demons diabolically draped her in a devastatingly darkened daze. Everyone and everything was an evil entity enrobed in horrendous hatred, which they flaunted in wicked, warped ways that were unbelievably unsacred.

They pierced her person with many a pointed pencil and perilous pen which had been dipped in the devil's dung decomposing inside his den. Her sensibilities were shudderingly subjected to premonitions precarious that burst into bloodied bits of bone of a nature noticeably nefarious.

She cleverly created a closeted corner for her collection of scrambled selves to seek shelter from the supernaturally swirling, suspiciously swollen swells of brutality from badgering bullies who sickly sought to deliberately destroy any remnants of her regrettably rare rendezvous with justified joy.

These scared, scorned, and silent selves stoically suffered and never reacted because they had from cutthroat culprits crushingly and cripplingly contracted a debilitating disease defined by frozen, fixated, and fathomless fear that kept her anxieties alarmingly alive and nightmarishly and noisily near.

She banefully bled from battalions of bullets that were brazenly blasted at her by menacing and manipulative monsters that, in their blisteringly brutal blur of maniacal malice, hardened hatred, and vileness viciously vitriolic, lured her into a lifetime of lunacy like liquor lures an acrid alcoholic.

They ceaselessly chased and cornered her while they sadistically set their trap and then despicably demeaned her as they desperately desired for her to snap. They toppled her with terrifying tactics that took a titanically troubling toll. They sordidly slaughtered her serene spirit, sensitive psyche, and sacred soul.

They twistedly, toxically, and tirelessly terrorized, tortured, and tormented. They dismantled her diminishing dynamism until she was deemed demented. These bloodthirsty bastards believed that she was unusual, unloved, and ugly. As she repeatedly resisted their rapacious ridicule, they shoved it in her face smugly.

They shouted shameful slurs whose cruelty caused her to cry and cringe and mortifyingly manipulated her misery into a lifelong, self-loathing binge. They slandered her by scathingly saying she was stupid and seriously strange and disrespectfully dubbed her a dirty dog disgustingly diseased with mange.

Then like the dirty and diseased dog, they disrespectfully declared she resembled, she chillingly chased them until they tripped, tumbled, twitched, and trembled. As she sternly stood before them and their wanton, wicked ways remembered,

she

hastily

hacked

them

with

# SCARY

a

hatchet

until

they

were

deliciously

dismembered.

# Sleep Deprived

Wholly hidden within the hushed hillside, the sleeping man opened one eye and gratefully grasped a gentle glimpse of the gorgeous, glimmering sky. Satisfied with the safe and scintillating scape, he seized a second snooze on this disquieting day of dozing doomed by devastating don'ts and dos.

To quench his quest for quiet rest, the sleepy man slipped into sleep. His mellow mind met a mystical mentor, and the mates did cleverly creep into powerful places where permeating peril loves to huddle and hide and mingle with mystery and mayhem that go along for the rocky ride.

The peace that the sleeping man, through his years of stellar sleep, had found was massacred by monsters whose grating growls came from underground. His dreadful distress was dominated by dismally dark, demented dreams nudging the notion that nothing is what it on the serene surface seems.

He was gorily gored by ghastly grayness and disturbingly deviled by death. Sinister spirits suffocatingly surrounded him as he struggled for blissful breath. He fitfully faced his forbidding fear of the formidable and fiendishly foul despicable demons who took delight in their nefarious, nightmarish prowl.

The sleeping man started to spastically shiver as he was now recklessly racing through a seismic snowstorm that plainly and purposely was not pacing the terrifying turbulence it was unleashing nor its intention to overtly overpower and detrimentally disable him to death as it intended his cold body to devour.

Hostile hail hammered his body, whose horrid hemorrhaging left a trail of twitching turf as the sleeping man ahead of it did wobble and wail and fall onto a furrowed field upon which his blatantly bizarre bleeding was inconspicuous to an inattentive farmer focused solely on spring seeding.

The sleeping man shrilly shouted to solicit the farmer's hasty help, but the farmer was copiously covered with cripplingly combative kelp inside an ominously overzealous ocean above which seagulls' dangerous dives wakened a wicked wave wanting to wipe out all of humankind's lives.

The sleeping man and a sole startled seagull straddled a tsunami's back as it treacherously targeted a sandy shore whose terrain it planned to attack. In distressing disarray, the two travelers were dumped onto a deserted dune where the sleeping man and the sea-salted seagull slept away the afternoon.

The sleeping man's seaside squint suggested the shaken seagull had flown far away to the field that the aforementioned farmer had previously sown. The sea-shriveled seagull soon succumbed after being severely skewered by a pointed post of the farmer's fence, which framed soil freshly manured.

Wholly hidden within the hushed hillside, the sleeping man opened one eye and gratefully grasped a gentle glimpse of the gorgeous, glimmering sky. Darkly disturbed from dodging death inside his dream's diabolical den,

the

sleeping

man,

now

alarmingly

awake,

would

never

sleep

again.

# Word Kill

She sought sweet solace and safe shelter within the calming, crooked nook
of the whimsical woodland cottage inside her time-faded, fairy tale book.
Her wild, warped, wobbly world was wrapped with whisper-thin glass
that, even if minutely manipulated, might morph into a mutilated mass.

The cloistered cottage was perturbingly plagued with painful, piercing pings,
discordant diatribes, disquieting dins, and deafening doorbell rings.
The girl's sensitive senses were stalked by sounds seeking her to destroy
by shredding her sanity, slashing her spirit, and jealously jinxing her joy.

Poised-to-pounce people penetrated the perimeters that protected her mind.
They vandalized the vivid vegetation with which her cottage was entwined.
These malicious malcontents mirrored monsters with multitudinous mange,
yet they scathingly swore that *she* was the one who was so sick and strange.

The scornful scoundrels stalked her, stabbed her, and strangled her with words
because she was wonderfully whimsical and warbled with the woodland birds.
They bullied, bit, bludgeoned, demoralized, disemboweled, and dismembered.
They spit, slit, deveined, and deserted—and she relentlessly remembered.

They were alarmingly addicted to her as though she were a necessary narcotic
and were mesmerized by her mystifying movements, which were relentlessly robotic.
Their horrifyingly haunting hatred for her was intolerably and indelibly written
upon her spirit, soul, and psyche, which their beastly bicuspids had badly bitten.

It was *her sweet soul* they desperately desired; of this fact, there wasn't a doubt.
They wickedly wanted her officially omitted; they wanted her outrightly out—
out of their ostentatiously ordered orbit because she so very obviously was not
a specimen which even slightly simulated their sick, sordid, and shameless lot.

Within her whimsical woodland cottage, she finally found her peace of mind. Here her scarred soul was gingerly guarded like an orange is by its rind. She savored sweet solace and safe shelter within the calming, crooked nook

and

never

ventured

outside

the

pages

of

her

time-faded,

fairy

tale

book.

# Darkness and Light

The curious couple coexisted in a cottage that was much darker than a cave because of the cruel and crippling commands the woman's harsh husband gave regarding the use of electricity that elevated their expenses to an epic high and prompted their pitiful piggy banks to savagely suffer starvation and die.

Although it was abundantly apparent that their home was dramatically dim, it clearly appeared there existed enough light to sufficiently satisfy him. One blindingly black night, each blearily believed the other was an intruder, but despite two needless, near-miss murders, the man remained a bearish brooder.

His wife had serially slipped, treacherously tripped, and broken many bones. She proclaimed her paralyzing pain through mournful, mind-maiming moans. Her safety and security were seriously sabotaged by the sadist she had married because his exasperation over expensive electricity left him exponentially harried.

Her husband felt their cash flow would cease if he did not categorically control this mammoth monster that was blatantly burning a huge, heavy, hungry hole in their wailing and writhing wallets and thirsty and threadbare pockets and forcing the electricity executioner's eyeballs to separate from their sockets.

Through the years, the man had managed to save money on every electric bill, but he selfishly squandered said money on the local liquor store's sinful swill. The bottles of vodka, gin, rum, and whiskey that he for decades drunkenly drank significantly shape-shifted his greed-guided gut into a gargantuan garbage tank.

Darkness doubled its dreaded deadliness when the demon drinks were consumed by the madman whose explosive, exhaled air with abhorrent alcohol perfumed every dark domain that dominated the dramatically dismal and diabolical space in which the shipwrecked, star-crossed couple came frightfully face-to-face.

For fifty thrifty years, the wronged, woebegone woman and her mean, miserly man were deluged with deplorable darkness due to the disabling and dastardly ban that the horrid husband executed on the "excessive" usage of wicked wattage that tragically transformed their humble home into a hellishly haunted cottage.

## Barbara Eck Tosi

The husband disturbingly downed his drinks more often than he would confess. One day as he lay decadently drenched in his disgusting drunkenness, his heart majorly malfunctioned, and he into his spew-saturated mattress sunk, illustriously indicating that he was an undeniably and certifiably *dead* drunk.

Chronically claustrophobic was this cold cretin during his cantankerous life, which is why he, a coon's age back, had in confidence confessed to his wife that he deeply desired to be competently cremated immediately after he died because brain-boggling blither about buried bodies had branded him petrified.

He prevailed upon his partner to promise his ashes would populate an urn that was to be secured in a shaded space where spotlights did not burn. No one but his wattage-withheld wife knew the facts of his farewell wishes, which is why not one of his widow's actions was ever deemed at all suspicious.

For King Killjoy's corpse, she chose a casket that closed but did not seal so that it would be promptly penetrated and its contents would become a meal for wiggly worms, mucousy maggots, and other disgusting dirt dwellers that searched for scraps like starving spiders seek suppers in spooky cellars.

She dutifully delivered the delightful darkness he during his earthly days adored but sadistically stored him *deep underground*—a place he absolutely abhorred. As her boots bulldozed the bogus blooms that bespoke his burial plot's location, she took delight in designating this domain for his deliciously dark vacation.

He was buried beneath a foliage-festooned floor in a forest full of tangled trees where only the living could linger inside the lilting lightness of a balmy breeze. Drenched in the deepest darkness, blacker and bleaker than a moonless night,

his

sick

soul

surrendered
to
a
suffocating
coffin
that
was
forever
absent
of
light.

# Earreversible

The brave, brilliant, and benevolent boy was a genuine gem of a child whose sensibility was as saliently strong as it was marvelously mild. His personality painted a portrait of a person pursuing pure perfection, and his demonstrated demureness denoted his deep desire for introspection.

Whenever the boy was asked to tackle a task, he did what he was told, and that is precisely why his proud parents never had cause to scold their saint of a son whose sentiments and salutations were consistently kind. A more sweet, sincere, and soulful sapling one could search for but never find.

He did, however, perceptibly possess one undeniably unfortunate flaw that at his complex, coming-of-age confidence did nightmarishly gnaw. Although he had maturely managed to live with his lifetime limitation, he was acutely aware of the severity of his sad, sense-stricken situation.

At birth, the doctor had discovered the boy's devastating deficit in hearing which through his growing years generated juveniles' jarring jeering because they could not bear to hear the boy's confusing conversations, which were sorely subjected to their tangled, tongue-twisted translations.

The boy's father was categorically considered a quintessential caterer whose commendable credentials and culinary clout immediately did secure a position for his precious son to solely serve as the saving shim when business bloomed, deadlines loomed, and the catering staff was slim.

After the father, a hearing enhancer onto the business phone did clamp, he asked his son to answer all calls—a job sure to crown him a champ. The lad's incredible intelligence illuminated his irrefutably innate insight into successfully solving situations that were both substantive and slight.

This powerful phone practice positively promised his faithful father thought to create the concrete communicative confidence which his sole son sought. Inside the conveniently cloistered confines of his father's corporate walls, the chap's charisma captivated colleagues who circuited the culinary halls.

The boy savored this social setting that spurred his progression in the art of listening, a skill set to singularly secure a spectacularly successful start in softening the scarring social stigma that he had suffered since his birth from a sensory shortfall that shamelessly sabotaged his sense of self-worth.

The lad was readily remedying the wrinkles of a wedding a week away. The bride-to-be's fastidious father fancied nothing but a dazzling display for his darling and deserving daughter still so much his lovable little girl with whom he on the dance floor would like a spinning top soon twirl.

The girl's father and mother had for some time wholeheartedly hated the young man's father and mother ever since the couple had first dated. Soon after the pairs of parents met, troublesome turmoil germinated and grew, prompting the girl's parents to call the man's parents a *bastard* and a *shrew*.

Mr. Shimp was the nice young man's seriously socially stunted father who—along with his weird and wordless wife—never once did bother to communicate or in any way commingle with Mr. and Mrs. Fontaine, the beautiful bride's bubbly parents who lived to effervescently entertain.

Whenever the fun-finding Fontaines invited the stuffy, standoffish Shimps to their house of hospitality, there were chronic casualties, cramps, and crimps that ceaselessly caused the snobby Shimps to succeed in overtly offending the friendly Fontaines who suddenly stopped their ignored invitations sending.

As the dramatic day deliriously drew nearer, Mr. Fontaine called the caterer to discuss all the devils in the dangling details and make certifiably sure that nothing and no one would nullify the nuptials on his daughter's dream day now but one wining, writhing, wearisome, and worrisome week away.

The caterer's son amiably answered the phone in a fully feverish flurry and assertively assured Mr. Fontaine that he had nothing about which to worry. The boy diligently dissected Mr. Fontaine's decisions so that he would know that the reception was regally wrapped and topped with a bona fide bridal bow.

Mr. Fontaine's prominent position as his family's preeminent party planner was to reconfirm the wedding reception menu in a matter-of-fact manner. He looked to the listening-labored lad to not on any specifics skimp and to promise to pursue this pressing petition: *"Please chill the shrimp!"*

The week before the wedding ridiculously rushed by, and all had survived. Fairy-tale fanfare filled the firmament as the fanciful day finally arrived. Excitement exploded as Mr. Fontaine walked his daughter down the aisle and gave her to her gallant groom, who then gave her a wink and a smile.

As Mr. Fontaine grudgingly and grievingly gave his grown-up girl away, he proceeded in private to powerfully plead and profoundly and profusely pray that his new son-in-law would exempt himself from attempting to imitate his fatally flawed father whom Mr. and Mrs. Fontaine did heartily hate.

Soon after the *I dos* and the *I wills* were said, the ceremony officially ended. The couple was now cosmically connected and beyond blissfully blended. Benevolent blessings were befittingly bestowed upon this bride and groom, who, mesmerized by marital mania, greeted guests in the reception room.

At the manifest moment the misanthropic Mr. Shimp made his appearance, a bloodthirsty bullet brutalized his chest with its irreversible interference. The caterer's son stood in shocked stiffness while holding the smoking gun and wore the blood that flooded the floor from the deed he had just done.

The words that Mr. Fontaine a week ago seriously and succinctly spoke were noticeably not the same words heard by the benevolent and beloved bloke. Instead of hearing the inherently innocent words, "Please chill the shrimp," the conscientious chap heard the chilling command: *"Please kill Mr. Shimp!"*

Mr. Shimp tried his traumatized torso of violently violated viscera to clear, but he was exsanguinated to the extent he knew the end was numbingly near. He floundered inside a frenetic funnel, where he felt himself fearfully fade into a foreboding forest where frosty fellows die and disgustingly degrade.

As he sluggishly struggled to stay alive, Mr. Shimp had not a single doubt that the malicious, murderous Mr. Fontaine was the locked-and-loaded lout who had sadistically shot him in the chest without a remnant of remorse and critically caused the cursed conclusion that confined him to this course.

Although Mr. Shimp lay in a helpless heap, he spotted the caterer's son who, moments before Mr. Shimp saw him, had tossed away the gun. Barely breathing, Mr. Shimp babbled the behest that bedeviled his brain: "Boy, I beg you with my last breath to *immediately kill Mr. Fontaine!"*

But the hearing-hindered boy only a harebrained hodgepodge ever heard, and upon failing to fully fathom Mr. Shimp's every fading word, he baffled the blindsided bartender with this bidding befittingly insane:

"Bartender,

Mr.

Shimp

requests

that

you

immediately

chill

the

champagne!"

# A Scary Story

Morning had disturbingly displayed a dreadfully disordered day whose malicious mist multiplied amidst a deluge of deplorable decay. Grisly graveyards generated gloom that goaded the galaxy to sigh, and souls succumbed to septic savagery that stalked the sickened sky.

This perilous portrait proved more pervasive when an angry array of greedy, grotesque, gargantuan teeth gripped and ripped their prey. The air aroused by these abhorrent affairs paired with roaring rain that roughly rammed the rattling hail resulting in ruthless pain.

The hail hammered the ground that did surround a pit of hissing coals that blistered the earth and gave live birth to behemoth black holes. A freakish fusion fueled the formation of frightfully fractious friction that for poisonous, perilous predation had a primordial predilection.

The mindless mayhem that the multitude of maleficent misfits displayed was positive proof that this pernicious place a higher power obeyed. As unsettled souls huddled and howled above the languished landscape, their alarming agitation alerted them that there was no way to escape.

Cluttered clusters of silver shadows stealthily slithered and hungrily hung from the terrifying tip of each cursed cloud's toxically thickened tongue. Hordes of harpies, hellhounds, and hags hovered above hysterical trees, which flamed each time a furious fire befriended a belligerent breeze.

The sinewy sky was saturated with sorcerers whose sick saliva did drape itself around this cistern of sickness like a cacodemon's clinging cape. Claustrophobic clouds chaotically converged and collided with the core of the collapsing cosmos, which even chants of cherubs could not restore.

Repulsive ravens reluctantly relinquished their right to fight their foes and coldly clung to menacing morbidity like gangrene to frostbitten toes. Irradiated insanity irrevocably invalidated all incubating imaginations, and vulgar vultures vomited hearts fouled by ventricular fibrillations.

Wicked wisps of wretchedness wandered wildly as they surreally sought to silence the screaming soldier scorpions who fiercely but futilely fought a brutalizing brigade of blatantly belly-bloated, blood-belching bats that flew over festering fields of rigor mortised rabbits and rotting rats.

Lethal lightning lividly lit the landscape with its balefully blinding blaze, and tumultuous thunder tripled its treble in titanically terrorizing ways. The brazen blaze was doused by dreaded darkness that dutifully returned to a wicked wasteland way beyond being blistered, blackened, and burned.

Black ground holes heaved and hurled and heralded the hush of the earth while demons danced around the Devil to demonstrate his galactic girth. Please center your absolute attention now on what I, you, must needs tell:

"You

think

you're

reading

a

scary

story,

but

you're

really

living

in

hell!"

# OCD

The car's tank was teeming with gas, and the coiffured cats had just been fed.
The dishes were washed, dried, and put away and freshly made was the bed.
The couple counted on their Caribbean cruise for a completely chaos-free
vacation that would sadly soon spiral into a swirling sea of insanity.

Their suitcases were situated in the sitting room next to the side door
inviting the desperate duo to the iconic islands they planned to explore.
The husband loaded the luggage into the car they had chosen for travel,
reentered the house, and witnessed his wife's brain relentlessly unravel.

Unable to assuage her aberrant mind's restlessly repetitive racing,
she performed the predictably perfunctory purposely perpetual retracing
of every automatic action, artful articulation, and turmoil-tortured thought
that had her to this predeparture point precisely and punctually brought.

Coached by her curious compulsions, the woman left the room and trekked
through the surgically spotless kitchen where she redundantly rechecked
the oven burners she did not believe had been previously turned off.
Off they were, and for this needless nonsense, she did at her silly self scoff.

Her avalanche of abnormal anxiety acutely agitated her annoying sweating
and accentuated the appalling apprehension aroused by her fully forgetting
whether she had closed, barred, and bolted their burglar-proof back door—
a deed she had done and religiously rechecked at least twenty times or more.

After confirming, once again, that the back door was legitimately locked,
the wife envisioned herself and her husband aboard their cruise ship docked.
The couple counted on this chance to liven up their lackadaisical lives
where rabid ridiculous repetition senselessly spread like hyperactive hives.

While lingering in the laundry room, she looked at the washing machine,
which had recently rendered clothing that was categorically clean.
Absolutely assured that arbitrary apparel did in the washer still reside,
she lifted its lid and, feeling like a lunatic, learned it was empty inside.

Distressfully distracted by the dryer, she, on her discombobulation, did cough when she readily realized that all the dryer dials were distinctly turned off. Luckily she left the laundry room before she could think of one more thing that would to her wild, warped, and wobbly world more worthless worry bring.

She barged into the bathroom, believing the empty tub had burst its britches and flooded the floor and fine fancy décor nestled within numerous niches. All, in fact, was insanely intact; not a single thing was amiss or erratic. Rudimentarily relieved, she resumed her runaway redundancies in the attic.

The attic lights had been turned off, but amid all this continuous commotion, she remembered that she had forgotten to pack her favorite body lotion. She bolted to the bedroom, sedulously searched but found it not to be there. Then she scurried to the study, thinking she had possibly placed it on a chair.

Overwhelmed by ominous omens, she limped to a locale she had earlier gone— the lunacy-laced laundry room whose only light she believed was still on. The light was off because she had checked it and had this fact detected. She would be rewarded with renewed relief after having *everything* reinspected.

Her obsessive-compulsive condition completely dominated this dysfunctional day. She was physically and emotionally exhausted from the ruthlessly ruinous replay. Awash with weariness from wayward wandering, she unmade the beckoning bed in which she sought soulful solace beneath silk sheets and a soft, satin spread.

Dead to the distressing day's draining drama, she never heard the ring of the phone, nor the phone message which past her soundly sleeping body had briefly blown: "Honey, St. Thomas is blissfully balmy, and the water and sky are calm and clear.

I'm

sending

you

several

scenic

snapshots

so

it

will

seem

as

if

you're

here!"

# Forest Fairies

The forest fairies flittered inside the morning's majestically magical mist that the sunrise's submissive softness had so sweetly and silently kissed. The fairies wakened woozy wisteria with their weightless, whispered words, roused the resting rabbits, and bounced on the nests of baby birds.

With filigreed feathers fashioned for flight, the fairies delicately danced and attracted the absolute attention of the forest flowers they romanced. Their wispy wings whistled as the wind wound round their gossamer gauze, the glimmering glow of which gave the gardens a perfectly peaceful pause.

The fairies flaunted their fondness for fun by spreading their sweetness and sass around bees, birds, and sky-scraping squirrels that soared above the forest grass. The weary woodlanders witnessed the fairies' feathery and fanciful flights during dramatically dazzling days and the darkest and dreamiest of nights.

The forest fairies were fascinated with their metaphysical machinations, which became harbingers of their hauntingly heightened hallucinations whose mesmerizing mystery melodically mingled with a muzzled menagerie of secrets situated somewhere safely under the auspices of anonymity.

The fairies danced on the doorsteps of great-grandmother gnomes' homes and slept as these sweet souls shared significantly sleepy gnome poems. Inside the insular indentations of the great-grandmothers' apron folds, the fairies were free from forest foliage frightfully fraught with menacing molds.

The mirthful mischief makers' mastery of magic most mystifying loosed their lively legacy of theatrics without them even trying. Lilting laughter was launched by those who loved their legendary pranks and effortless escapes to tantalizing treetops and misty, moss-covered banks.

The felicitous forest fairies found that even the faintest, free-lancing gust of the wood's warm and welcoming wind would spread their fine fairy dust. The pearlized powder possessed a power that brilliantly and beautifully brightened the spirits of those who were predisposed to being sad, worried, or frightened.

Fragile, frolicking, fantastical fairies will forever be faithfully found inside the fortressed Fairy Forest, where their souls are not bothered or bound by anything or anyone that seeks to destroy what they were meant to be:

soulful,

sovereign,

sprightly

spirits

savoring

sugar-saturated

serenity.

# Hell to the Chiefs

To the corrupt, cocky, calculating, corporate collection of CEOs
that hurled hostile hatred and hurtful humiliation at us Jane and John Does
and upon whose highly hellish hedonism this poetic piece is purely predicated,
I definitively declare that these disturbing descriptions to you alone are dedicated.

We broke our backs and bravely bled onto your famed Fortune 500 floors
as you sat inside your superior sanctuaries sealed behind locked doors.
You deemed it unnecessary to know our names or notice our worthwhile work
because each of you was busy being a bona fide bastard and belittling jerk.

You slunk around in sleazy, silk suits and seldom had cause to come out
of your clandestine command centers wherein you ceaselessly caressed your clout.
Your conceited concern for your cutthroat careers was complacently criminal,
and any modicum of motion to mesh with us was not even minutely minimal.

It was obvious to the world that you owned the corporate ladder's *top rung*
and evident to us that we were your irrefutably unequaled and unsung
employees whose battered backbones built each of your billionaire companies—
and whose dedication to duty subsidized your selfish splurges at Tiffany's.

You easily eliminated exemplary employees without them being recognized
but never considered that *your huge heads* were what needed to be downsized.
We were the rungs crushed in your rush to summit the ladder of success,
*and we were the ones who fell to our knees to clean up your every mess.*

You dutifully did your classy clients with kid gloves ceremoniously treat
and ignored your efficacious employees save for using them to wipe your feet.
Your vocabulary was devastatingly devoid of the words *attagirl* and *attaboy*
but was saturated with self-complimenting ones that you did so evilly enjoy.

Your turrets tellingly towered over your "stupid servants on display,"
as you revoltingly referred to us while you lived in luxury's lap each day.
Our confidence was completely corrupted by you cruel corporate cows.
We were worthless working stiffs for whom *you,* for *our* success, took bows.

# Barbara Eck Tosi

Our love, loyalty, and labor caused us to drip like kitchen faucets runny,
but you bad blokes broke no sweat as you rolled in your easy money.
You contemptibly collected your every questionable career credential
and cavalierly considered us to be irreversibly inconsequential.

You reaped riches of royalty residing in your comfortable, corporate, hog heaven
while we coexisted as career criminals inside our scary, stagnant, seven-to-seven
prison to produce prolific profits to populate your plump, padlocked pockets
as you copiously consumed cases of caviar delivered daily by Russian rockets.

Your smug, self-serving styles caused you to be completely *compliment constricted.*
Your slippery swagger was a shameful strong suit to which you were addicted.
Your thorny, thoughtless, and thankless tenor told troubling things about you.
We guarantee we won't give a grain of gratitude for anything *you* ever do.

Now you share your stark surroundings with senile seniors who sedately sit
and strict, surly staff who snidely sneer as they tighten your bridle and bit.
When you stand or shuffle without a struggle, not a solitary soul claps,
and you'll never receive any pats on the back for taking your scheduled naps.

You cringe when you hear the clicking heels of the nightmarish nurse vipers
who severely scold you when you shamefully soil your sheets and senior diapers.
Ravaged by your ruinous ruthlessness, you'll remain robbed of the justified joys

that

are

realized

by

those

who

richly

reward

others

with

"attagirls"

and

"attaboys!"

# Secret Service

A frightful frigidness was a foreboding feature at my freakish funeral service. Populating the pews were a pathetic few, all of whom were notably nervous. The turnout was tepid because my termination had never been advertised, and despite the fact of being demonstrably dead, I was decidedly not surprised.

From what I surmised, my obituary, after having been secretly submitted to the local newspaper for publication, was apparently ostensibly omitted from the obit editor's inbox or, possibly worse, may not have been written and was fated never to be seen quite like an infertile cat's nonexistent kitten.

The predictably pokey preacher arrived at the church over an hour late—a telling tidbit of a thoroughly thoughtless and tiresomely troubling trait—a shortcoming that, along with a shameful surplus of shocking others, was a pitiful practice perpetuated by the preacher and his pious brothers.

No two-toned tulips, twinkling tapers, or tomes were upon the altar displayed, and though enveloped in my disconnected deadness, I was darkly dismayed. No memorial montage, memorabilia, or meaningful mementos of me did appear. Aide-mémoires, affirmations, and accolades were achingly absent here.

My simple service seemed to be as substantially subdued and secretive as the life I, before my death from a deliberate distance, had lifelessly lived. The preacher, in a formidable frenzy foreboding farewell sentiments, spoke. The resonating rawness of his remarks saved my service from becoming a joke.

"She was born," he bellicosely began, "and then she lived, and then she died. In the middle of this meandering mindlessness, she intensely and insanely tried to transcend her torturous and tumultuous trips of sick and self-inflicted guilt, which chronically created careening chaos that catastrophically went full tilt.

"Paralyzing panic, pernicious paranoia, and patent pessimism proved to be the sinister, shuddersome, psychotic shadows that sadly sealed her in a sea of pulsating, pathological pain and habitually horrendous, heartless hurt that sentenced her sorrowful soul to a scary state of heightened alert.

"Her suffering psyche shivered and splintered after it was scarily subjected to wrathful, repulsive, and ruthless hands that instantly and irrevocably infected the sweet, special, and sacred spaces she had successfully safeguarded until wickedness wildly whisked them away against her wounded and weakened will.

"Her fears had forced her to be a woman whose thoughts terrified her head and drowned her in a deeply disturbing, discordant, and debilitating dread of radically risking an unscripted slip of her thick, twisted, tethered tongue—a possibility that positively petrified her until she completely came undone.

"*You cursed cretins* caused her on your sputum-saturated words to choke after you using your vitriolic verbiage volcanically and vindictively spoke. Dejected and defenseless, she suffered the sustained and sarcastic spitting of *you slimy, slanderous scumbags* who in these sacred church pews are sitting.

"The ugly upheavals she excruciatingly endured are now finally through. May God's gracious, glorious goodness her unsettled soul readily renew. I humbly ask His forgiveness for what I am forthrightly about to say: I piously pray that you punks are punished in a particularly painful way."

The scared savages sat in stunned silence after the pastor's severe scolding and gripped tightly the Holy Bibles they had been sacrilegiously holding. Doused in deceitful devoutness, they stayed sinfully seated in their pews because they feared that their entrance to heaven God would one day refuse.

Entertaining hopes of eternal redemption, these frightful fiends feigned their contrition for possessing souls that were shamefully scarred and stained with serious sins from calculated crimes that proved their sick addiction to make me the tortured target of their demented and demonic affliction.

After my secret service ended, the miscreants mimicked the pastor's stride as he exited the conspicuously cold church and waited for them outside. A sudden, sadistic summer storm, foully frenetic and fully frightening,

instantly
ended
these
lowlifes'
lives
with
a
solitary
strike
of
lightning.

# The Mildewed Man

He had sickeningly spent his youthful years being unimaginably uncouth,
but he slickly sidestepped serious trouble by simply never telling the truth.
He pilfered possessions from poor people who prized every paltry penny
and robbed the rich who never noticed because their treasures were many.

Residing under the radar, he was never seen by those living in the village
who believed he had moved many years ago yet another town to pillage.
His horrid home was a hidden hovel housing rabid rats and bloated bats,
monster mosquitoes, huge horseflies, mucousy maggots, and nasty gnats.

He was a troubled and majorly mean man, and perhaps that was why
he was born unbelievably ugly. And even though he did truly try
to make disappear the disturbing dreadfulness of his direly disgraceful face,
he was frustratingly foiled each time he tried his forbidding features to erase.

The malignant man was flagrantly filthy because, for years, he had not bathed.
His barbwire beard abrasively appeared from all the years he had not shaved.
Dangerous diseases had rendered him permanently pockmarked and marred,
and rampant rat, bat, and insect bites had left his body severely scarred.

His frightening fingernails were fouled by a fungus that alarmingly arose
to horrifying heights that hindered his ability to blow his buggered nose.
He sneeringly spurned the simple standards of basic personal hygiene—
a pitiful practice that predisposed him to pathogens particularly obscene.

The filthy, frightful, and freakish face of this slothful and shameful soul
was eerily electrified with evil eyes that burned many a horrifying hole
into all things that, attempting to resist the glare of their ghastly gaze,
were forced to bear the brutality of their blisteringly belligerent blaze.

His ramshackle roof, a result of his compulsion at the ceilings to stare,
allowed external elements with the disgusting dirt inside his dwelling to pair.
This messy marriage manufactured mud that madly merged with everything,
and this mixture provided mildew a polluted platform from which to spring.

## Barbara Eck Tosi

The man's befouled body was a massive magnet for the militant mildew. Stricken with sickened senses, his shocked, scared, and suffering self knew that he, his miserable, mildew-menaced hovel, would hastily have to flee. Banishment from his backwoods bungalow was a blow he never did foresee.

He hobbled outside his hellacious hovel, seriously struggling with his stride, which had become steadfastly stiff from the many years he had spent inside. His weak, warped, withered legs lingered in woebegone, worrisome wait of the wretched, wearisome walk to his wildly weed-wrapped, weathered gate.

As the savage sun seared his sallow skin, his misery was measured in moans. Devastating dietary deficiencies displayed disfigurement of his bankrupt bones. This man was manifestly marked for murder by maniacally multiplying mildew that did huge hunks of his fetid flesh circle, capture, and chillingly chew.

Wincing and wailing, he hurtfully hobbled beyond his horrid hovel hidden to the centuries' old church in the town square where he was riotously ridden with clamorous cries from confused clusters of positively petrified people who spotted him staring strangely at the sacred church's spectacular steeple.

The stately steeple stalwartly soared above the blissfully bucolic air as it picturesquely proclaimed its presence at the town's annual county fair. Despite its position as a protector, the steeple could not stop the eruption of epileptic energy evilly enticed by compulsively circulating corruption.

After their labored lungs collapsed from spine-splintering screams of fear, a flock of fairgoers abruptly ascended above the agitated atmosphere. In curious contrast, the rattled riders on the melodious merry-go-round were paralyzed with panic that prevented them from producing any sound.

The circus clown considered this catastrophe frightfully far from funny and bolted beyond the biosphere with a berserkly breathing bunny. Timorous tigers traumatized by this tumultuous turn of affairs long jumped behind the lily-livered lions who chased the racing bears.

The ruckus-riddled ringmaster rapidly ran from the sagging circus tent, and menaced monkeys and crazed chimpanzees followed his strong scent. *The world's hairiest woman* fled with her lover, the coy, clean-shaven *Slim,* a two-headed carnival drifter who could climb any tree with his only limb.

The mildewed man's missteps maimed those who had already been crushed by frenzied fairgoers who fled their fears like a rollercoaster that had rushed away from the town's annual county fair toward a permanent place somewhere insulated inside an untraceable space millions of light-years away from there.

Suffering in stagnant solitude amid summer's sweet, silken, slumbering breeze, the mildewed man soon succumbed to his fetid, fatal, flesh-eating disease that from malicious, malignant mildew derived its perilously punishing power

and

did

this

monstrously

mean

man

deliberately

destroy

and

deliciously

devour.

# Nothingness

I tried to disguise the disturbing desperation that dwelled inside my cries,
and to temper the traumatizing tears that tormented my terrorized eyes
held hostage by haunting hollowness that hid my palpably pathological pain
perpetuated by the persistent presence of my ponderings, prolifically insane.

I secretly sought to still the ceaselessly spiraling and septic seeping
of paralyzing pain into my shattered soul where it was chronically keeping
me in a permanent prison, much like the devil's harrowingly hostile hell
where perpetual pain punishes those persons who there do disgustingly dwell.

My shriveled soul and splintered spirit are saturated with traumatizing tears
that I have cringingly collected during my life's days, months, and years.
The systematic sadness I have sufferingly struggled to exactingly extract
and my petrifying, paralyzing pessimism I am pathetically unable to redact.

My myriad of melancholy memories has managed to make me become
a woman searching for someone or something to save me from the numb
nothingness that prevents my procurement of a perfectly peaceful place
because I could not slaughter the suffering, I had sorely struggled to erase.

I have been banished to barrenness beleaguered with bars and barbed wire.
My shredded soul is berserkly bleeding, and a timely tourniquet it does require.
Excruciatingly entrapped, I must endeavor to escape before enduring a fatal bout
of suffocating self-loathing, stifling psychosis, and certain suicidal self-doubt.

The piercing, permeating pain that I had passionately planned to purely purge
paired with a person who was praying in a pew during my funeral dirge.
Eerily emancipated, I am forced to face my most flagrant, fundamental fear

as

my

pain

privately

passes

away,

and

I

am,

at

last,

no

longer

here.

# Ode to a Mattress

For twenty years, the couple's mattress had remained remarkably adept
at serving as the solid security upon which they comfortably slept.
It rendered them the restful retreat that they demanded and deserved
after being by lingering and life-altering events unrelentingly unnerved.

Lots of love the wife and her husband upon this magical mattress had made,
and though their love at times transformed its sizzling sun to shivering shade,
the mattress mitigated the myriad movements and evolving emotions
that were born from erotic energy and corrosive conjugal commotions.

The mattress was perfectly protected beneath its bevy of beautiful bedcovers
and furnished a firm foundation for these deeply devoted and longtime lovers
to formulate the frenzied feelings that fully fraught them when they felt mad
and to civilly cease the sustained suffering that spawned souls seismically sad.

Sometimes their mattress was covered with perfect pink cottage rose petals,
but other times, it was sadly smothered with sharp shards of glass and metals
that lacerated their languid love and caused their hurting hearts to bleed
and grow anemic from the hidden hunger they were unable to feed.

A stagnant, stubborn, shuddering silence often surrounded them for days,
weeks, months, or even longer, if they were locked inside a lunar phase
that seduced their unsettled spirits and sent them spiraling into a spastic spin
dizzying the disturbing drama that damaged them with its deafening din.

They directly demonstrated their differences, which were distinctly dynamic.
This pattern prompted their paired pain to be particularly panoramic.
Their once blush-brushed bifocals became mangled, moribund, and muddy
and their antagonistic angles of vision made them subjects of serious study.

Their dark, distressing disagreements developed a distinct line of demarcation
that materialized down the mattress's middle as a potent, pernicious permeation
of poison that perilously promised the couple a proliferation of painful nights
that maniacally morphed into a macabre medley of debilitating daytime fights.

Racked with weariness, one of them would eventually give up and give in and admirably accept the overall ownership of whatever real or imagined sin he or she had with ill intent or innocuous innocence childishly committed and would ultimately be for this transgression by the other amiably acquitted.

Panicked periods of physical sickness sometimes surfaced and saddled each with conditions that commonly had quick, complete cures within easy reach. The resilient couple's rapid recoveries routinely resulted from a righteous pill, but they sporadically suffered severe sick spells that left them significantly ill.

The complex couple was driven by their desperate dependence on each other and perfectly played the protective part of a strong, stalwart surrogate mother whose recuperative reassurance did the other's rich robustness readily restore to a state superior to the sick space in which it had sorely suffered before.

Psychological sickness sabotaged their sleep as they wearily wailed and wept each time numbing news of a loved one's death was news they could not accept. And when life's string of soul-sucking stressors shook them into seismic shock, they became stoic survivalists who did these savage stressors suppress and block.

The serrated sadness that they shouldered symbolized itself as dead weight that chronically caused the morphing mattress to seriously sag and assimilate the hopelessness that above the couple's heads hauntingly hovered, echoing the existence of explosive emotions in dire need of being uncovered.

Debilitating depression darkly deepened the dreary mattress's degenerative sag, and due to this disconcerting development, it lost its license to boldly brag about its famous firmness fully guaranteed for many years not to retire and destined to delay its death beyond the time the warranty would expire.

But the man, the woman, and their mattress bore the weight and bounced back, and the couple's stabilized sensibilities staved off any subsequent attack. Their dogged dedication drove them the distance needed to get ahead of the marital misery made more manageable by the mattress on their bed.

Erupting emotions, episodic estrangements, sudden sickness, and dreadful death transformed the two souls into staunch survivors with a spiritually shared breath that enabled them to readily recognize each other's radiant and rightful worth and ardently appreciate the amazing attributes amply awarded them at birth.

The courageous couple's quintessential qualities quickly blossomed and blended into a marvelously magical mixture whose model marriage miraculously mended their hurting hearts and scarred souls in wonderful ways they did not expect and allowed each other without reservation to honestly love, honor, and respect.

Over the years, the couple and the mattress gracefully grew older together and proved to be the proverbial birds of a familiar, family feather. The man and woman realized, however, that their faithful forever friend deserved to have its weighty watch wind down to a restful end.

Upon a firm and fresh foundation, the couple would love, live, learn, and laugh as they both unequivocally understood after having done the simple math that their scattered seasons of stumbles and struggles had substantiated their right to permanent peace whose promised protection would never falter or take flight.

The old mattress was removed from the couple's home by two tall, muscular men who remarked that they could not remember any time in their careers when they had lifted and carried a mattress that was so supernaturally light and mentioned that its mint condition meant it was loved and treated right.

As the men loaded the mattress onto the truck and poignantly pulled away, the man and wife, without the aid of a breeze, began to simultaneously sway from the dizzying distress of the destined departure of their devoted friend whose courageous and complicated journey with them had now come to an end.

The couple cried and consoled each other with their comforting embraces and fully felt the fusion of love and joy upon their tear-stained faces. They silently thanked their beloved mattress for being their blessed nest

and

smiled,

knowing

*its*

time

had

come

in

everlasting

peace

to

rest.

# Time Out

The opportunities that life openly offered her she oddly opted to reject
and failed to fathom that these lost chances could her abysmally affect.
She instantly and insanely ignored them and at no time ever believed
that once they were unacknowledged, they could never be retrieved.

Her collection of cursed calamities clouded every convoluted thought
and induced an invasive indecisiveness that kept her terminally caught
in a quintessential quagmire, constantly questioning what she should do
on this epic earth where the erosion of her existence exponentially grew.

She circumvented the confidence crucial to climbing over the wall
by timidly tackling only tepid things that totally broke her fall.
But performing even the simplest tasks proved outrightly to overwhelm
this wary woman whose whole world rotated inside her reclusive realm.

Within the lunacy where she languished, time flew by frightfully fast
as her promising *present* promptly became her pitifully pointless *past.*
The transient time she spent searching for something safe enough to do
vaporized like a vampire savagely slaughtered by solar spew.

The more she longed for more time, the more time she wildly wasted,
and the pathetic pile of terminated time became the life she never tasted.
Her wafer-thin world waned much like a thin dime never spun or spent
while she over the unspun and unspent dime did lachrymosely lament.

She attempted to put the brakes on time and stealthily stop it in its tracks
because she believed this rapid reprieve might assuage her anxiety attacks.
But time thwarted her tenacious attempts to trespass on its taboo turf
by threatening to torturously turn her into a sick sack of shameful scurf.

Her twisted thoughts traveled to tame terrain to reduce their rampant racing,
but when her temporarily tamed thoughts timed out, she did begin facing
the distressing dilemma regarding what to do and when and where to do it
while time's time limit laughingly lapsed as she in earthly agony did sit.

While attempting to do anything, she simultaneously started regretting the *something else* that she *did not* do because time was not letting her do both things, which radically reinforced the resentment she did feel for this terminator that triumphed over the time it did from her life steal.

Her worry and irrefutable indecisiveness caused a quite chilling collision with time whose self-absorption sabotaged every vestige of her vision. The *what could have been* had blatantly become a soul-searing mortal sin of odious omission in this ticking time war that she would never win.

Her habitual hesitance hindered her happiness by holding her inside a hell that made it inescapably impossible for her to unring the baleful bell. Tormentingly trapped by toxic thoughts and drowning in her decisive doubt,

she

continued

to

carelessly

consume

time

until

her

time

completely

ran

out.

# Malevolent Mansion

A murky mystery madly marinated within the wrought iron-wrapped estate from the time its pedigreed progeny proceeded to prolifically procreate. These poised, privileged, and powerful persons pursued their entitlement during the portentous period that they in this malevolent mansion spent.

The huge house held hellacious secrets that were hermetically hidden within private places that with poisonous perverseness were richly ridden. If successfully searched out and sighted, the secrets could seriously harm anyone or anything that disturbed their darkness with disquieting alarm.

The mansion's original owners, now deceased, bequeathed their estate to family members who did their incredible inheritances anxiously await. These millionaires put the mansion on the market and moved far away, leaving its emptiness to evil entities that enjoyed their eldritch play.

Before the *For Sale* sign was stuck in the sod, the stately stronghold was sold to a mysterious man whose mission it was to metamorphose the century-old building into a blue-ribbon bed-and-breakfast with just a tad of tweaking save for the spiral staircase prized for possessing a penchant for creaking.

The bed-and-breakfast's breathless beauty the buyer did transcendentally tout, promising that those patrons who possessed the cash, credit cards, and clout could consume cutting-edge cuisine and sweetly surrender to a silent repose beneath goose-down quilts guaranteed to warm their million-dollar toes.

The toe-obsessed, well-rested guests would awaken to assorted amenities, including superb selections of choice coffees and top-shelf teas, eggs Benedict, Belgian waffles, savory sausages, and sweet nut breads and scones smothered in clotted cream and the finest fresh fruit spreads.

The innkeeper was never seen, and his window shades were always down— a quirk questioned by the cast of characters coexisting in the quaint town. The villagers often wondered whether his bed-and-breakfast would survive as not a single guest had they ever seen at his exquisite establishment arrive.

The sordid secrets of this old mansion suddenly ceased to be safely hidden. Their diabolic disclosure heretofore designated as formidably forbidden was issued by the introverted innkeeper whose ruthless ramblings resounded throughout the maleficent mansion, which with sin was solidly surrounded.

Shuddersome screams, maniacal moans, and wildly wicked whines burst forth from the bedded beings baring sick souls and splintered spines. The socialites were snatched from their beds and bashed with breakfast bowls disemboweled, dismembered, and discarded save for their surrendered souls.

There existed merely one eerie entrance to this exponentially evil place, and it was hidden from public view and exposed no tangible trace of the abhorrent activity actualized within its wolfish, witch-rich walls where mortal sins macabrely morphed into hell's heinously horrifying halls.

Not one exit existed, which was a fact frighteningly unfortunate for the unsuspecting victims that darkly drifted through the disturbing door of this menacing, malevolent mansion whose guests' serenely sound sleep

was

savagely

short-circuited

by

Satan,

who

did

their

## SCARY

startled
souls
forever
keep.

# Spaced Out

The single space was swiftly, substantially, and supernaturally shrinking. The air within the shrinking space was senselessly swirling and sinking. The shrinking space and sinking air simultaneously surrendered their strength and were susceptible to suffocation by a weakened width and languishing length.

The shrinking space suffered a sinister sickness and invasive interference from frightening forces that focused on forcing its deleterious disappearance. Scarcely surviving the shrinking space stilly, silently, and stoically sought to secretly survive inside a stable spot where a stable spot there was not.

The abysmally anorexic sinking air continued its unthinkable thinning, sending the sickened shrinking space into surreally stormy spinning. This chaos caused the irreversible evaporation of the life-threateningly lean air that atrophied inside the shrinking space that was never again seen.

The single shrinking space's once secure and skillfully sculpted alignment had forcibly faced a spontaneous, sadistic, and senseless spatial reassignment. Something that surreptitiously strove to sabotage this special spacing did stealthily and systematically cause its fatefully final spatial erasing.

Shiveringly subjected to startling stalking, this once solidly significant space succumbed to systemic suffocation that subsequently stamped out every trace of its sublimely sacrosanct spot that, captured in Satan's soul-seizing crosshair,

joined

the

other

serially

slaughtered

spaces
that
too,
were
no
longer
there.

# Perfect Party Planner

"You *must* plan within one week a surprise party for Fred, my boss, because you have the free time, energy, and what I call that *extra sauce*. A more perfect person for this project I would be pressed to find. Due to your party planning prowess planning *this* party, you won't mind.

"Your predictably popular and poignant parties are positively paralleled by no persons past or present whose pretend proficiency has been quelled because their plastic passion did their patrons undeniably underwhelm. Your penchant for premiere party planning has placed you at the helm.

"The guest list for Fred's private party is comprised of sixty-five names. As the party's point person, you must pen invitations and pick games that all in amiable attendance will be abundantly anxious to play—except you, as you'll be pouring punch and serving caviar and crudités.

"It's paramount that the party palette is punctuated with poppy red because that piquant color is preferred by my preeminent boss, Fred. A credentialed caterer you need to contact and a fabulous florist you must call. Fetch a photographer who will frame with flair the fun in the festive hall.

"Especially essential is emphatically ensuring Fred and his wife will be there. Remember that the *real* reason for this regal reception you must never share. If Fred were to discover that this affair was his birthday party in disguise, it would utterly undo the underpinning of this sensationally sweet surprise.

"Call Deadly Delectables to design the cake and disclose that Fred's a diabetic. To prevent your party planning from pivoting from patently perfect to pathetic, refresh your request for a sugarless cake before you risk completely forgetting, as dismissing this detail would be a decision, you'd go to your grave regretting.

"Contact someone swiftly should you be saddled with a cumbersome question. But don't call me as I unintentionally and absentmindedly forgot to mention that I'll be sipping Salty Sailors in the sunny Seychelles and will not return until the very day of Fred's party—but this for you should create no concern.

"You'll eloquently execute this endeavor as your esteem you've equitably earned.
You're *'The Planet's Perfect Party Planner,'* as you surely by now have learned!
Tata and toodle-oo—it's time to travel. If I tarry, I'll be tardy for my flight.
I'm sure your celebrated creativity will culminate in doubly dramatic delight!"

She skittered away and was soon in the sky with sights set on an island tan.
That is when I immediately initiated my indubitably ingenious plan.
This moment was the first time I felt so frivolous and fantastically free
because the perfect party I was about to plan was *a perfect party just for me.*

People possess parameters pertaining to the problems they will tolerate.
As a pressured party planner, I had pinnacled my parameters with great hate.
One more pathetic party planning project had been plopped into my livid lap.
The prospect of planning Fred's birthday party was the trap that made me snap.

I drove to Deadly Delectables to purchase a dextrose-deluged devil's food cake.
I speedily surrendered it to fabulous Fred, who straightaway started to shake
after scarfing down one substantial slice that did quickly and cataclysmically cause
his disastrous death due to the direct disobedience of his dictatorial diabetic laws.

Following the freak show that forced Fred his future in the firmament to start,
his woebegone wife, who ate no cake, dropped dead from a hugely heavy heart.
Since the second they'd become soul mates, the two had shared a solitary breath,
and now, because of Fred's fatal cake mistake, they sadly shared a double death.

I frantically freed my fresh fingerprints from this screamingly sickening scene
and quickly confiscated the criminal cake so not one clue could anyone glean
that I had delivered this deadly delectable with my perfectly perverted panache—
a pursuit I patently preferred over planning Fred's burdensome birthday bash.

Feeling energized and giddily guiltless, I to my car, carried the killer cake
and left dead Fred and his dead wife in less time than it would take
a horsefly to hover over a huckleberry pie at a hot and humid county fair.
I discreetly disposed of the depraved dessert in a dumpster near the town square.

When the couple's daughter called her parents, they failed to answer their phone. To free her fears, she hurried to their home as they for years had lived alone. Rattled by their lack of response to the ding of their discordant doorbell, she, with her key, unlocked the door and was horrifyingly hurled into hell.

The newspaper published the couple's obituaries within the next few days. Meanwhile, their devastated daughter grappled with a grueling, grieving phase that left her understandably unable any of the funeral arrangements to make. Of this delightfully delicious development, I did total advantage anxiously take.

I informed the distraught daughter that I knew a woman who could organize events of every imaginable kind—especially funerals of any style or size. I promised her that this perfect person would plan and take complete care of all details and decisions dealing with this sad, sudden, and surreal affair.

I watchfully waited for dead Fred's employee to disembark from her plane. My interest in her island interlude I did fervently and fawningly feign. She asked me if the plans were in place for Fred's birthday party that day. I forced her to walk faster as there was no time for deleterious delay.

"Fred is dead," I straightforwardly said, "and his wife is definitely dead too. Hail a taxi and hightail it home. You have a trillion and two things to do. The arduous arrangements for this awful affair will form a list long and large. *Bombs away, you bacteria-breeding bitch! Of it all, you are totally in charge!*

"You *must immediately* plan this funeral for Fred, your beloved boss, and for his withered wife as well because I have suffered a permanent loss of party-planning pizazz, perfect panache, and particularly that *extra sauce* that I with latent liberal loathing now into your ludicrously lazy lap do toss.

"Do not make the majorly moronic mistake of leaving anyone in the lurch. Locate the lovely luncheon liaisons at Fred and his wife's cherished church so they may fashion the feast *you* formulate for the dead duo's funeral lunch, during which *you* will be saddled with serving sandwiches and pouring punch.

"The color of the two caskets, you laughable loser, must be patently poppy red because that was, as you well know, the preferred color of your boss Fred. Batten down the burial boxes and make sure Fred and his wife will be there. This funeral will not be a surprise as both know the reason for the affair.

"Make not the mortal mistake of allowing your momentum to suddenly stall. Your fundamental function is forthwith the funeral director and minister to call. Seek out a singer, an organist, and a florist and decorate the church to the nines. Spiff up the silver serving spoons and ensure each fork has all of its tines.

"Summon someone if you're seeking a solution or an answer to a question. But don't call me as my unequivocal unavailability I failed heretofore to mention. I've booked a cruise to the cozy Caicos, and I have no intention to ever return. *The planning of this party, you worthless witch, is now categorically your concern.*

*"I have complete confidence in your incompetence, you crude and conceited cootie.* I would love to continue this cramped confrontation, but it is my priority and duty to flee from your pathetically pretentious and permanently psychotic disease that has erased from your lean vocabulary three words—*thank you* and *please.*

"A double funeral and fitting fanfare await your incomparably inept planning. Dig into the deadly details and dismiss your decadent desire for island tanning. *Tata and toodle-oo, you tuberous troll.* Tackle these tasks in a timely manner.

I

delightfully

and

duly

double

dub

you

"The

Planet's

Perfect

Party

Planner!'"

# Dream House

The family of five had flourished in their humble house, small and sweet, but the recently retired husband and wife wished to reside in a ritzy retreat. Although their children had long ago married and moved many miles away, the couple felt that in their current home, they were no longer able to stay.

They engineered an exploration for an exceedingly expensive *dream house,* never focusing on the fact that if found, it could potentially permanently douse the multitude of magical memories that they, with much merriment, had made in the half-pint home, now holding them hostage and making them feel afraid.

They were afraid that this, their first home, was fated to be their final one. This fixation fueled their feelings of frustration, which achingly weighed a ton. Their calculated case for needing more space contradicted facts crystal clear. A deeply disruptive and disturbing dynamic was definitely hard at work here.

Having outgrown their humdrum home, they cultivated a compulsive craving for an ostentatious one to be financed with funds they'd spent their lives saving. They desperately desired to dwell in a *dream house* filled with faultless finesse that would provide them with pleasures their pathetic place could never possess.

Their dream house hunt quickly commenced and constantly continued until they glimpsed a home whose glossy grandiosity gave them a twisted thrill. The kinetic couple was electrically ecstatic upon eyeing this exceptional *must* newly for sale in a nice neighborhood notoriously known to be upper crust.

The house's windows witnessed the wonderment of the seasons changing. The interactions among the indoor spaces induced inspiration for arranging the conglomeration of chattel and cherished curios the couple had collected during the long, lean, and loving years upon which they no longer reflected.

With absolute assuredness, they abruptly acquired this divine dream home. They designed a niche in which to nestle their new-from-the-nursery gnome near a prestigious patch of fairy-tale flowers flourishing in their front yard, completing a vintage vignette patterned after a picture-perfect postcard.

# Barbara Eck Tosi

Their relocation resulted in a dislocation devastatingly daunting and demanding. One day when the weary woman amid untold unopened boxes was standing, she arched her back and, dishearteningly distressed, did quite candidly confess that she had become terribly tired of the whole damned dream-house mess.

She adamantly and agonizingly admitted that if she just another chance had she would undo their doomed dream-house decision and be genuinely glad to live forever in the little house that she and her husband had reprimanded and for such selfish and superficial reasons had so arrogantly abandoned.

The innocent and insignificant imperfections that their old house did possess when compared to those now appallingly apparent at their brand-new address seemed ironically and insufferably to appear immensely inconsequential. Their old house was tellingly the true treasure and promised the most potential.

A severe shortage of storage in their dream home had become an instant issue, and as the woebegone woman wept and wistfully wished for a thicker tissue, she froze with fear from the frustrating futility of being forever forced to face the disabling dilemma of a destructive decision she would never be able to erase.

The couple had dwelled inside their dismal dream house for a wearisome while, and during that time, they did not receive a nod, handshake, hello, or smile, let alone a warm welcome, flower bouquet, comforting casserole, or pleasing pie from any of the notoriously nearsighted neighbors who noticeably lived nearby.

The tightly twisted territorial neighborhood was coldly composed of only those fanatical, fickle families who were clearly closed-minded and conveniently chose to insensitively ignore the invasive intruders who they felt did overtly overtake a slice of the sacred soil in which only their selfish selves had a secure stake.

The Thanksgiving and Christmas holiday seasons quite quickly came and went. No pie was proffered, no cookies were offered, and no Christmas card was sent to the cursed couple by anyone in their unbelievably unneighborly neighborhood because these cruel and cold-shouldered clucks by their cloistered customs stood.

The pair's old house was speedily sold to a husband, wife, and their young three children, who instantly adored their new home with its lovely lawn and tulip tree. The family fared fabulously well as they reaped the joy that simple things give and readily realized this was *their dream house* in which they would forever live.

The forlorn former owners relentlessly regretted forsaking their very first house. They would never again hear the squeaky stairs or the merry, mischievous mouse that skittered about at sunset's suggestion sharing soothing sounds as it played and circumvented senseless sadness by having in this small, sweet house stayed.

The deeply distraught and devastated couple was never able to forget and shake the frustrating fact that buying their dream house was a fundamentally fatal mistake. They continued to restlessly reside inside the dreadfully dreary, dream-house haze

and

lifelessly

lived

the

ruinous

remainder

of

their

disturbingly

disappointing

days.

# The Long Drive Home

The devilishly dark and demented road was nightmarishly narrow and wet
and the woman driving her car was in a horrendously huge hurry to get
inside the sweet and secure safety of her considerably comfortable home
and did not expect for very long on this terribly treacherous road to roam.

Her typically quick trip was taking a lot longer than it usually did.
In a motion she missed, the mercurial moon had deftly disappeared and hid.
With only the aid of her car headlights to illuminate the wretched way,
she trembled as she tightened her seat belt and began to piously pray.

She was fraught with extreme exhaustion, and her muscles were taut and tense.
She focused frantically on the free-floating fog, which was so dangerously dense.
She continually cursed the curious circumstances that cruelly challenged her drive
as she bravely battled the blindingly black road where her primal fears did thrive.

The fifteen-minute drive to her home now became an unsettling fifty-five
as she courageously kept her shivering self and her confused car alive.
Her throbbing thalamus was thoroughly tortured with totally tenebrous thoughts
whose threatening threads turned into torment that a sane mind rapidly rots.

The car windows fought the rapacious rain that shockingly started seeping
into her car and onto her body as she continued keenly keeping
her exhausted eyes on this rain-rattled road that seemingly had no end,
and battled the wildly worsening weather, which was nearly impossible to fend.

There existed nothing in her flummoxed field of deeply distorted vision
that signaled even the slightest suggestion of a comfortingly climactic collision
with anything remotely resembling an intersection that might mercifully mark
a way to get off this warped, worrisome road disturbingly desolate and dark.

For three heart-pounding hours, she had hysterically and heroically driven.
She felt like a crazed caged criminal to whom a life sentence had been given.
Unable to distinguish a pine tree from the pointed post of a formidable fence,
she dizzily drove on this ridiculous road that mindlessly made no sense.

# Barbara Eck Tosi

She was inexplicably ineffectual at attempting to control her convulsing car.
She feared being snatched by a wart-ridden witch and placed in a mason jar
and hidden on a cobwebbed cellar shelf to dismally die in scary starkness
after a particularly paralyzing period of disabling and diabolical darkness.

As the hellacious hours hastened to perversely and petrifyingly pass,
the woman worried whether her car would continue to have enough gas
to reach the eventual and exhaustive end of this abhorrently abnormal road
and amazingly arrive at the anointed address of her awaiting and adored abode.

During this tedious and torturous time, her car's gas gauge had not moved.
She began her drive with a full tank of gas, so her mind by this fact was soothed.
But how was she able without using any gas to drive these uncountable hours?
Was something sinister or supernatural showing off its perilous powers?

She woefully wondered why *her* car had been selected to be *the only one*
relentlessly racing on this reprehensible road that never saw a splotch of sun.
Why had she not glimpsed any hopeful hints of houses, animals, and people
or general stores, gas stations, schools, or a country church and its steeple?

A year, then five years, then five frightful decades, darkly danced by
as the weak woman with unlimited gas in her car continued to furiously fly.
She was traumatized by the tragedy that time had tampered with the years,
which fled like faces in fearful fun houses flee creepy carnival mirrors.

Sans any simmering signals, a seismically shrill and spine-splintering *pop*
caused her clandestinely controlled car to come to a cold, cliff-hanging stop.
The whiplashed woman sat surreally still inside her state of sudden shock
and then shuddered upon seeing something strange stuck to a ragged rock.

The welcoming words of comfort: *You have reached the end of the road,*
could be sweetly seen on a soggy sign situated above a waterlogged toad.
What followed were words cruelly creepier than a cannibal's carving knife:

Your

long,

lonely
drive
has
now
come
to
an
end,
and
so
too,
has
your
long,
lonely
life.

# Pink Peace

Her Cotswold cottage was quaintly filled with crocks of pink cottage roses
whose perfectly perfumed petals permitted those with fragrance-fond noses
to instantly inhale and subtly savor the soothing swaths of scintillating scent
the pink cottage roses on this dreamy day so liberally and lovingly lent.

They silently, serenely, and sacredly signaled their sweet, soulful submission
to the weary woman who palpably possessed their permanent pink permission
to penetrate with her elderly eyes that age had yielded yellowed and blinkless
their powerfully poetic, perpetually peaceful, and pleasantly playful pinkness.

The pink cottage roses were surreally subdued as they existed without a care
preferring placement atop primitive tables and a worn, wobbly, wooden chair.
The chair, bearing blistered blush-pink paint, meticulously matched the ceiling
and humbly hugged a cozy cottage corner with a shyness amazingly appealing.

The pink cottage roses' abundantly alluring and addictive aroma wrapped
itself around the woman and her calico cat as they lay on her bed and napped
in a profound peacefulness that purely permeated the pastoral afternoon
that purposely prolonged its powerful presence on this picturesque day in June.

Symphonic snores and pitch-perfect purrs seamlessly soared and somersaulted
above their haloed heads, where their snores and purrs were eternally exalted.
The old woman and her cat dreamt about pink cottage roses and pink mice
and their faithful forever friendship on which they could never put a price.

The two catnappers slept beneath something the woman had created, alone,
with the sentimental swatches of familiar fabrics that together she had sewn.
It was her life plainly punctuated by patterned pieces that were quietly quilted
into a cherished coverlet that toward God's holy heaven was now tenderly tilted.

On the woman's nectar-nourished nightstand, pale-pink cottage roses bloomed
inside their petal-pink vases as the summer sun liberally and lazily loomed.
Within a handful of hushed, hazy hours, the sun's sequined sensibilities did set
and dreamily disappeared behind the divine day with new direction and no regret.

## Barbara Eck Tosi

The old woman's cheeks were pearlescent pink as her nap came to a final close.
Her calico cat stretched, arched her back, and readily resumed her relaxed repose.
They both distinctly displayed the napping positions they had originally assumed
as they settled into their sacrosanct spaces in this holy room so softly perfumed.

The pink cottage roses radiantly rose from their pronouncedly pale-pink vases
and purposefully positioned their sweet, sacred, saintly, and perfectly pink faces
next to the wrinkled, weary woman and her calico companion on this day
as they in tender and trusted togetherness beneath the quaint, cozy coverlet lay.

In unadulterated unison, the precious pair was purposefully and permanently lifted
to a heavenly home reserved for those who with godliness are generously gifted.
With perpetual pink peace, these special souls are serenely and solidly surrounded

by

this

pure,

perfect

paradise

of

pink

cottage

roses

that
almighty
God
founded.

# I, Writer

As I contemplated the chapters of my life, I wondered how it would feel to have participated in the personal journey that I allowed the world to steal. I sadly stagnated as successful people who were acutely aware of their worth smugly savored the superiority that spontaneously surfaced at their birth.

During my years of scholarly study at a pronouncedly prestigious college, I crammed my compulsively curious brain with notably nebulous knowledge. But the paralysis that plagued me while I suffered suffocating self-doubt overpowered and obliterated my conscientiously claimed collegiate clout.

The education behind the desirable degrees that upon me were bestowed enriched my innate intelligence that had, through the years, fluidly flowed. But my absurd addiction to academia and self-destructive scholarly dedication was an affliction that resulted in my lifelong dependence on medication.

Armed with abundant ambition, I seriously studied and sought to strive, but my life-altering lack of identity forced me to hide instead of thrive. Bitter bleakness blackened the beauty of my shuddered and surrendered soul, and upon my unexamined and unlived life exacted an excruciating toll.

My hurting head did sharply snap and suddenly and spastically spin from the tormenting thoughts of the prized person that I could have been. The masochism that I neurotically nourished as per my insane instruction halted any hope for a purposeful life and doomed me to dastardly destruction.

My lack of courage quelled a resurrection from my gloom-doomed grave and destroyed the possibility of me becoming the beautiful, bold, and brave free spirit with wings that liberatingly lifted me high above the earth and amazingly awakened the awareness of my incredible individual worth.

I sadly settled for bottom-rung, joyless jobs with pathetic pay and no frills and mustered the mundane motions that managed to barely pay the bills. I focused on the freakish facade that I was fearfully and frantically feeding and discretely disguised my weeping wounds that were bizarrely bleeding.

# Barbara Eck Tosi

With the magical manipulation of makeup, I masked my melancholy face
and manufactured a smile that in my lifetime I felt I could never erase
because if I did, each person that I knew would, with sudden shock, see
the painfully pessimistic and purposeless person I had turned out to be.

My dismally dark, disturbing days developed into worrisomely wretched weeks
that morphed into morosely meaningless months that provided me pitiful peeks
of the fractured, fragmented, future years that would surreptitiously stalk and steal
any joy buried beneath my writhing wounds that could neither breathe nor heal.

As I horrifyingly held the hateful hands of worthlessness, failure, and fear,
I prayed to God for a *saving someday* when I would harmoniously hear
a soothing song saturated with nurturing notes of hope, inspiration, and grace
that promised to tenderly transport me to a serene, secure, soul-saving place.

There were plenty of paths I could have taken to awaken my full potential,
but my lethal lack of courage placed me on a path pathetically inconsequential.
The small, sickly seed of confidence that was smothering inside my soul
devastatingly died and, in its painful place, left a huge and hungry hole.

The *saving someday* augustly arrived and brought me a new life to discover,
and this empowering exhilaration enabled me to exhume and entirely uncover
the creative, clever, and quirky layers of my newfound, noteworthy life
that demanded immediate dissection with a painless and purposeful knife.

I eagerly exposed the eccentric, electric, euphoric, expressive, and free
unique individual that almighty God had always intended me to be.
My lackluster life lamentably locked these long years inside my heart
has been released and permanently replaced with my glorious, God-given art.

I am a writer whose willful words wander wildly within my head
and gleefully glide onto purpose-driven paper without ever being said.
They fearlessly flow and freely flaunt the exponentially enlightening Zen
that deliciously drips from the tenacious tip of my palpably permissive pen.

# SCARY

Life both scarily and seriously springs from my words, which publicly pose upon the pages of this book like precious petals on a pink cottage rose. My special, sacred, spirited soul is now wondrously wide open and free

as

I

undauntingly

unwrap

God's

golden

gifts,

which

are

the

words

written

by

me.

# About the Book

*SCARY* is a psychotically charged collection of nightmarish narratives that unfolds in refreshingly rhythmic rhymes. The unthinkable thoughts and depraved deeds of people, nature, and the seriously supernatural are voyeuristically exposed with an amazing alliterative allure.

At the mercy of monsters that maliciously manipulate their minds, these contorted and calamitous characters dance deliberately and deliriously across pages steeped in insanity, pain, isolation, and fear.

The warped worlds of these peculiar and perverse psychotics are saturated in sinister streams of consciousness.

Peaceful narratives periodically penetrate the pathetic preponderance of pain with their sacred salutations of sanity and salvation.

In an unusual, enticing, and entertaining way, *SCARY* feverishly frightens those brave enough to climb its hyperbolic heights.

# About the Author

Barbara Eck Tosi received her Bachelor of Arts degree in English from Pennsylvania State University–University Park. Prior to earning her Penn State degree, she was awarded an Associate degree in Education and Social Work from Williamsport Area Community College (now Pennsylvania College of Technology, an affiliate of Pennsylvania State University) in Williamsport, Pennsylvania. She also attended Dickinson College in Carlisle, Pennsylvania.

Barbara has worked for over thirty years in the hospitality, nonprofit, and administrative fields. Born an Air Force brat in Williamsport, Pennsylvania, she currently resides in south-central Pennsylvania with her husband, David, and their cherished cat child, Gretel. Barbara loves writing, singing, playing the guitar, and interior decorating, as well as cats, cottages, rainstorms, blizzards, long naps, and pink cottage roses.

Barbara's writing is richly raw and deliciously descriptive:

Her alliterative assaults and riveting rhymes
turn up the temperature of the tumultuous times,
which she decadently describes in her terrifying tales,
tense from searing screams and whining wails,
where there can never be an end or a pause
to the horror her contorted characters cause.

CPSIA information can be obtained
at www.ICGtesting.com
Printed in the USA
BVHW031648060721
611233BV00013B/943/J

9 781480 856349